SOMETHING MORE SPLENDID THAN TWO

Fig. 1. Detail from Hieronymus Bosch, *Ship of Fools* (1490–1500)

First published in 2022 by dead letter office, BABEL Working Group, an imprint of punctum books, Earth, Milky Way.
https://punctumbooks.com

The BABEL Working Group is a collective and desiring-assemblage of scholar–gypsies with no leaders or followers, no top and no bottom, and only a middle. BABEL roams and stalks the ruins of the post-historical university as a multiplicity, a pack, looking for other roaming packs with which to cohabit and build temporary shelters for intellectual vagabonds. BABEL is an experiment in ephemerality. Find us if you can.

ISBN-13: 978-1-68571-064-4 (print)
ISBN-13: 978-1-68571-065-1 (ePDF)

DOI: 10.53288/0412.1.00

LCCN: 2022947564
Library of Congress Cataloging Data is available from the Library of Congress

Book design: Vincent W.J. van Gerven Oei
Cover image: Felipe Baeza, *Ahuehuete*, 2018. Ink, graphite, twine, glitter, egg tempera, and cut paper collaged on paper, 59¼ × 44 inches. © Felipe Baeza. Courtesy of Maureen Paley, London

punctumbooks

spontaneous acts of scholarly combustion

HIC SVNT MONSTRA

Something More Splendid Than Two

josé rivers alfaro

p.

Contents

Acknowledgments

I am fortunate to be in relationship with many special people who make me and this work possible.

Thank you to my students at UC Riverside, Moreno Valley College, and Cosumnes River College, for teaching me how to write again.

Thank you to Vincent W.J. van Gerven Oei and Eileen A. Fradenburg Joy at punctum books for supporting my writing and for all the incredible work you all do to make scholarship open access. Vincent, I truly appreciate the care and labor you put into the book designing process.

To my early educators, who made me want to teach, thank you for changing my life. Special thanks to Paula Turner, my eighth-grade English teacher, for turning me into a reader. I am grateful to have been radicalized by you. To Mr. Valdivia, my fifth-grade teacher, thank you for modeling softness and gentle masculinity at a time in my life when I needed it most.

Thank you to my mentors. To Jennifer Doyle, for creating enduring communities of care, for your unending kindness, and for sharing this work with your circles before I believed it had earned a readership. To Emma Stapely, for your close listening, always, and for the co-conspiring joys I experienced with you while thinking and writing in friendship.

To Sarita Cannon, for the table, the cookie, and the heart you shared with me at the Fog Lifter Café in San Francisco seven years ago. Thank you for years of being a comrade, a spirit lifter, a listening ear, a friend of my mind, a believer of my writing. My love for you is abundant. Look. How lovely it is, this thing we have done together.

To the women of color at Cosumnes River College who opened a path where there was none before. Thank you to Lisa Abraham, for holding up a mirror to show me that I could call myself an artist. To Tonya Williams, thank you for inviting me to dream with you. To my colleagues at CRC, thank you for always treating me as a person first. Special thanks to Kathryn Mayo, for supporting me and every medium of art I pursue.

Thank you to my Riverside queer sisters for holding me: Sarah, Chelsea, Hannah, and Angelica.

Sarah, I feel fortunate to write beside your heart.

Thank you to Patty, for sharing a dwelling with me in friendship and for suggesting that I write more about the ideas that came to make up this book.

To all my dance communities in Riverside, San Francisco, and Sacramento, thank you always for bringing me back to my body.

To my brothers, in their search for the feminine within, thank you for showing up with love and laughter.

To my father, thank you for your nonlinear love and for a childhood fueled by music.

To the extra set of parents who at any point claimed me as their son: Nina Marti, Nino David, Chuy, y Miguel, thank you for embracing me.

To my maternal grandfather, Jesús Macias, mi tito, thank you for every carefully woven story you told on Sundays at the dinner table. I learned from you the importance of memory and storytelling.

To my primas, the sisters I grew up with, thank you for turning me into a feminist.

To my cousin Rosa, whom I admire in many ways, thank you for showing me how to be brave, for modeling what it means to honor our pasts, our ancestors, our histories. Thank you for feeding me with dance, food, wisdom, and love when I left home to join SFSU with you. I am blessed with the comunidades you gave me when I was healing from the shame I inherited in this country as the queer son of Mexican immigrants.

To my lifelong friend Amy, for your partnership and illuminating compassion in my life. To James, for your generous spirit, and for reading my manuscript with care.

To Javi, for your magic. For the platicas that challenge me, the hugs that feed me back my breath, the serenatas in the morning. For the thoughtful love and warm patience you practiced as I wrote this. I feel incredibly lucky to share this timeline and precious encounter with you. I continue to make my journey home dancing beside your light, querido.

To the women from where I emerge an outline: Maria de Jesus y Maria Elena, my grandmothers, thank you for the maternal love and sacrifice that lives on and survives even when the generations after you cannot always see it, y aunque todavía no lo comprenden. To my mother, María Guadalupe Macias, whose love my language makes a futile attempt to measure, your love is a tenderness not even diosito could have anticipated. Te amo, mama.

for my mother tongues

I was named after my father, but I write this
book under my pen name,
josé rivers alfaro

my last name finds its latitudes within the
Spanish phrase *al faro*
translated it means *to, or toward, the lighthouse*
my first name derives its meanings from
Hebrew and Spanish origins
translated it can mean, *he shall add*

adopting rivers as my middle name
my pen name reads
he shall add rivers to the lighthouse

"Still, like water, I remember where I was before I was 'straightened out.'"

— Toni Morrison, "The Site of Memory"

Prelude

Before we begin, tell me about the last time it stopped raining.

So it began again in the pages of John Rollin Ridge's book *The Life and Adventures of Joaquín Murieta*. As myth would have it, Ridge says que en aquellos tiempos the Mexican bandit hero, Joaquín Murrieta, crossed the us–Mexican border a year after foolish fathers drew it and tried his fortune during the Gold Rush. Hurt by the unruly state of violence and political turmoil his forefathers had created in northern México, the young Joaquín migrated from Sonora to Alta California with hopes that he would forget the men of his homeland and encounter a different if not better character in American men. Joaquín's hopes for a more peaceful and prosperous life were immediately destroyed, however, as he and his companion Rosita navigated a geography increasingly structured around anti-Mexican violence. The white American men he first met after crossing la frontera brutalized him and gang-raped Rosita after he refused to leave his claim. After resettling further north, his newly acquired farm was taken, and he was forbidden the right to mine for gold. While these first experiences certainly marred Joaquín's soul, his third and final wounding at the hands of American men served as the tipping point of his transition from noble man to bloodthirsty outlaw. Having borrowed a stolen horse from his half-brother, Joaquín one day found himself surrounded by an angry mob who charged him with theft. Without any due legal process, they tied him to a tree and publicly whipped him before they proceeded to lynch his half-brother. From then on Joaquín committed to a life of revenge and bloodshed. His soul, they say, took on the shape of a cavernous wound, a mouth, a bullet hole clamped wide, emptied. Without laws that could protect him, Joaquín took matters into his own hands and sliced, split, lacerated into the bodies who humiliated him. He formed an organized network of Mexican bandit men and women who would murder Anglo-Americans, raid their farms, and steal their horses. They say Joaquín was a master of disguise and nobody in California could identify or catch the man behind the gun and knife. Paranoia spread.

One day, upon returning to Arroyo Cantua, the periodic dwelling place where Rosita and the other bandit women remained tending to the stolen horses, Joaquín attempted to catch his reflection in the now dried-out creek but only saw his shadow. There in the clay he studied the faceless outline of the man he had been made. By then Joaquín had not just stopped at killing white men; he had, like them, also slaughtered Chinese miners, lowly Mexicans, and California Indigenous people along the way. Running his fingers through the holding place where desert water should have been, he waited until the sunset stretched his shadow horrifyingly close to the men — the fathers — he loathed on both sides of the border.

Some versions of the story say that it was not Joaquín, but his ruthless right-hand man, Three-Fingered Jack, who did most of the blind killing. It is the history of many men, after all, to escape accountability. The truth, really, if you are to believe Ridge's version of the story, is that by then you couldn't tell the difference between Joaquín, his bandits, and the men that were after them. In 1853 the state of California issued a reward for Joaquín's capture and hired Captain Harry Love and a lynch mob of white supremacists to find the Mexican organization. Near the edges of Arroyo Cantua, where the water still bleeds every spring even when the arid climate dries out the canary creek bed, they decapitated Joaquín and severed the hand of Three-Fingered Jack. Both head and limb were preserved in separate jars of whiskey as a spectacle for all of California to see. It is said that the floating head, the disfigured hand, could have belonged to any Mexican man. Because only the women know.

A Million Openings: The Reader's Queer Map

The legend of Joaquín Murrieta has many beginnings and many have tried to retell the tale of his life accurately. After having read multiple serialized newspapers, corridos, and oral histories traveling across California at the time in which the famous bandit lived, Cherokee writer John Rollin Ridge wrote his version of the story and in 1854 published the first novel written by a Native person, the first novel published in California, and the first American novel to include a Mexican protagonist. Since its publication, Joaquín's story has been retold again and again. Sometimes he is Zorro, sometimes he is Robin Hood of El Dorado, sometimes he is Batman. Each source disagrees about how the story begins; each source makes its return to the multiple mouths that spoke and sang Joaquín into existence before Ridge put it into writing. And in each new beginning of the story told long ago in the past and once again in the present, the retellings attempt to find the original wound that turned Joaquín into a violent man.

For Mexican American readers, the myth of Joaquín is used to explain the origin of our wounding as a people in the US. By rescoping the myth within this context, Joaquín has been cast as the symbolic father of the Chicanx movement before such an identity was put into language. Redeployed as a story of wrongs committed by white men after the border was drawn and the Treaty of Guadalupe Hidalgo was signed, Joaquín has become foundational for declaring 1848 as the beginning of Chicanx history. The boxer, writer, and leader of the Chicanx movement,

Rodolfo "Corky" Gonzales most famously announced *I am Joaquín* in his 1969 eponymously titled nationalist poem, heralding the vigilante as a popular hero Chicanes should look up to. Through Joaquín, Gonzales could claim that "THE GROUND WAS MINE." Because the Treaty of Guadalupe broke its promise to treat Mexican men with equal rights to own property, as Chicanes "Arrogant with pride / Bold with machismo / Rich in courage," the scattered Joaquíns living across the US would reclaim annexed lands to build a glorious Chicanx nation they would one day call Aztlán. Within the Chicanx imaginary, Aztlán represented the historical and mythic homeland the Aztecs allegedly inhabited before Spanish and Anglo conquest. Gonzales's poem does not directly mention Aztlán, but his representation of Joaquín as a mestizo with the blood of an "Aztec prince" contributed to mapping Chicanes as the rightful sovereigns of the Southwest by appropriating pre-Columbian Indigenous identity.

In the versions Chicanes tell, I can feel the loose ends of Joaquín's life that have been stitched up too neatly by this utopian nationalist narrative. I can feel how, out of fear, we leave out the failure of us, the ongoing war in us that I know continues to be left by the wayside, unremembered. And because we are afraid, we use up Joaquín's life; and none of us is more free. We want to forget that while Joaquín may have avenged the white Americans who hurt him, he also, as John Rollin Ridge remembers him, failed to hold and carry others in his geography of freedom. I have been reading John Rollin Ridge's version again and I am haunted by an old question that emerges from the possibility that Joaquín could have lived: *What if Joaquín never fell prey to patriarchy?* The question emerges from reading the violence Joaquín and his men direct against the women in their own band alongside the brutalities they also commit against other Mexican, Chinese, and Indigenous people of color, and so there is an imagining I have for another story I want to tell for Joaquín, *an other* life and death I want to write for him with words I do not have. Despite my wanting, I've been terrified to rewrite the tale, to imagine something else for this man who is trapped inside a story we keep on telling with the same beginning and end, because I fear the detour my memory might take. Somewhere within me, I know, is a wounded place, un-examined and silent, desiring and intent to remember him as he did not live, to forget him as he died. You see, the story of Joaquín is not really just a story. His life is hardly a life at all. It is an inventory of historical pain that precedes me and that has dug its way, passing in and through my body, a sieve of time. I have longed my entire life to forget how I've been marked by the myth of Joaquín. Which is another way of saying that I've let his story keep on telling itself without me. Which is also to say, I've attempted before to forget my immigrant Mexican father who also attempted to forget his father and so on. I've attempted to forget how the generation of men in my family have failed to hold one another across time and space and yet, while reading the story of Ridge's Joaquín, I remember what I had long ago buried deep in the pages of this story for someone else to find. The forgetting surfaces, rises from the memory I read beneath Ridge's landscape, and as he remembers how Joaquín and his men dominate and wound other men, I remember my father and my grandfather. And I am afraid of forgetting how our wounds are shared. And I'm afraid of forgetting to remember how we have failed each other.

Earlier, as I began retelling you the story of Joaquín's life as told by Ridge, I took you to the scene of Joaquín looking for his reflection in the water of the arroyo where he died. Ridge didn't actually write that part. I imagined it as a reader of his book. I imagined that Joaquín wanted to see himself reflected in the arroyo. But instead of encountering the image of himself in water, he sees only the now dried out clay bed. He thinks that because he doesn't see himself reflected back that the water is no longer there and that, without it, he is unable to remember his story. But the water is still there, giving him a story both un-derneath the clay and in the (in)visible markings it made on his body and the land. To see the water, he must remember what re-mains under the surface beneath his feet. It's possible the image of Joaquín at the arroyo appeared to me as I read Ridge's book and felt my reflection fall apart the longer I held my gaze on his Joaquín. I could sense, on the margins of the text where I felt the stories of my father and my grandfather haunt me, something written underneath the story that was upending me from time and space. This readerly feeling, this process of losing myself on the map of Joaquín's life, opened as I turned backwards in time to face the histories of colonization and the onset of failed solidarity that the writer, John Rollin Ridge, and the Cherokee men in his family experienced a long time before Joaquín or my father crossed the border.

At times, while stubbornly imagining that there might be another timeline for Joaquín's life, I have wondered whose story I am telling first: Joaquín's, my father's, mine, or John Rollin Ridge's. I have wondered which one of us is Joaquín. Although I am not Cherokee and although Ridge is not Mexican, reading Ridge's life as a part of the story of Joaquín tells me that we are connected not by shared cultural heritage or biological descent but by shared histories of colonized patriarchy and failed solidarities that have shaped our lives as racialized readers and writers. Our language is a watershed of blood and ink shedding, our tongues, confluences, coming together in alternative kinship to tell the story again. What feels important to me as a reader of his book and life is that I not equate my experience with his through direct identification, nor conflate Indigenous with Chicanx experiences, but that I trace how our intersecting inheritances at the margins of time offer a strategy for unpinning ourselves from the territorial and biological trappings of patriarchal identity. I want to bring together our positions — Ridge's and mine — as readers of the myth of Joaquín Murrieta, along with our differing memories of failed solidarity between the colonized men in our families, as a three-dimensional coordinate where our time zones can rub together and, from there, imagine a feminist reading practice that opens up as much space as possible for collective movement, healing, and imagination. I believe that in telling the histories of the Ridge men and those of my father as also a part of the Joaquín myth poses a serious challenge for Chicanes and Latines that continue to reproduce geographies of domination and exclusion. It strikes me that while Chicanes have clearly drawn from Ridge's text to imagine a future for themselves in the US, we have not engaged how the Cherokee histories surrounding the text might contribute to how we understand ourselves in relation to Indigenous communities and the land we currently occupy. Because Ridge is not Mexican, or perhaps because he is not an "Aztec," he troubles the geography of Aztlán and makes it float like an unlocatable chinampa. His life reminds us that the ground was not ours; that shifting beneath us are multiple Indigenous relations we continue to cut off in the past and the present. To remember Ridge's life in the undercurrents of Joaquín's story is to give up 1848 as our wound, to relinquish defining ourselves by a shared raza, and to give up finding ourselves on the map so that we can imagine kinships not based on blood, territorial borders, or national recognition, but by ongoing fluid relations. By doing the work of reading the myth of Joaquín collectively with Ridge, we Chicanes might lose ourselves from a patriarchal timeline that was never meant to hold us or liberate us; and instead, we might practice building, to borrow Toni Cade Bambara's term, a collective *gathering-us-in-ness* that opens from examining a wound of shared time that has no single beginning.[1]

---

1   One can never approach Chicanx and Latinx study in the same way after seriously engaging the work of Black feminists. My critiques of Chicanx nationalist identity and mestizaje, and my theorizations that instead call for Chicanx fluid relations across time, are deeply rooted in the Black feminist tradition and indebted to Black feminist work like Toni Cade Bambara, "Foreword to the First Edition, 1981," in Gloria Anzaldúa and Cherríe Moraga, *This Bridge Called My Back,* 4th edn. (New York: SUNY Press, 2015), xxix; Audre Lorde, *Zami: A New Spelling of My Name* (New York: Crossing Press, 1982); Sylvia Wynter, "1492: A New World View," in *Race, Discourse, and the Origin of the Americas: A New World View,* eds. Vera Lawrence Hyatt and Rex Nettleford (Washington: Smithsonian Institution Press, 1995), 5–57; and Hortense J. Spillers, "Mama's Baby, Papa's Maybe: An American Grammar Book," *Diacritics* 17, no. 2 (1987): 64–81. I have been particularly shaped by Wynter's foundational essay, which disrupts "1492" as a date that is used to fix narratives of European–Indigenous encounters that erase African diasporic histories, timelines, and perspectives in the Americas.

The reader of this writing should know now, before they continue reading, that this is a story about failed beginnings and that the story of Joaquín I here sit down to write to you will fail multiple times to begin (as I already have). The reader should also know that in each version of Joaquín I tell neither Ridge, my father, my grandfather, or I come out as heroes. The story I am telling you opens, instead, from the place of me reading John Rollin Ridge read the life of Joaquín, where, in that opening, the timelines of our collective failures unsettle and make our future moving together possible. The helix of time that fills my imagination with alternative futures for Joaquín maps a collective sojourn for the reader, a dancing movement José E. Muñoz described as *queerness*:

> We can understand queerness itself as being filled with the intention to be lost. Queerness is illegible and therefore lost in relation to the straight minds' mapping of space. Queerness is lost in space or lost in relation to the space of heteronormativity.[2]

To feel lost in the world of Joaquín's story is to allow the possibility of entering multiple past futures with no beginnings or ends. By losing Joaquín and ourselves in queer time and space as he travels, never settling in the familiar destinations we might have known him, our wounds open us up to worlds of solidarity we have kept ourselves from finding beneath our reflections.

Wounded men wounding wounded men wounding wounded men wounding.

Wounds travel. Open without beginning. Joaquín died in a wound. Arroyos are life-sustaining cuts in the earth. Flash floods travel down slopes and hillsides until the surface of the earth, churned, breaks to hold more running water. In this way,

---

2   José Esteban Muñoz, *Cruising Utopia: The Then and There of Queer Futurity* (Durham: Duke University Press, 2009), 72.

the water gives the land its new shape. When the creek bed dries during summer months, or when the land turns desert, looking eyes believe the land is barren, that its broken skin has never been touched by water. But those who trust the land, see the water even when it is gone; they know the water will return to the arroyo, to the wound, and will cut it deeper next time. They know, as the wildflowers know, that a desert is the visible absence of water that has yet to lay its tongue to rest. Joaquín's story is like that. There is a winding and wounding path back to where the water once was, where we can give shape to ourselves beyond the ending of Joaquín's story. The soil is still fertile, the scattered and dormant seeds of poppies and brittlebush waiting to bloom, in waiting to scatter a thousand timelines for more life, for a million blooming openings before they die to live again.

1

Joaquín As My Father

I had heard the myth of Joaquín before, or one like it, many times, out of the mouths of many men. The version I know best, however, is the one translated out of my mother's mouth, where Joaquín is my father, only his name is Jose Luis. At the age of eighteen, my father flees the small town of Atecucario, México in 1987 to make something of himself, to discover a life and fortune on the other side of the US–Mexican border not bound to men like his drunk and abusive father, Luis. Somewhere not here, he hopes, there is a place where money-hungry men do not come home drunk stumbling in the midnight hour having gambled the day's earnings. Somewhere not here, he thinks, there is a place where mothers do not wake the next morning to sell the last of their children's food.

In the memory he is fleeing, my grandmother María Elena joins other mothers chanting in the plaza of Atecucario to feed their families, ¡Tamales a tres pesos! ¡Tamales! ¡Gelatinas a dos! With what money my grandmother gathers, she will be able to purchase enough pan dulce y leche para el almuerzo. Si alcanza, para cenar, she might acquire tortillas de maíz, chile jalapeño, frijoles y queso seco from la tienda de esquina para la cena. And if it has been a successful year, which is rare, she will have enough left over to think beyond hunger and starvation to bargain for telas to patch her children's pants for the new school year and she will purchase enough pairs of huaraches for her eight growing children. The eldest children, Rafa, Leti, Gloria, and Chila will pass their worn torn ones down to Hilda, Jose Luis, Genaro, y Miguel. The new huaraches gifted to the eldest children will be a size too big and they will do their best to make them last long treks to school, soccer matches in el campo deportivo, muddied summers in pelting hot rain.

On the day my father decides to leave Atecucario for los estados unidos, he bites into his last handmade tortilla con frijoles y jalapeño that he will later long for but had for years grown tired of. He tells himself he is leaving for his mother, but he is leaving to forget the pain. He is leaving to forget his mother in the outdoor brick kitchen as she kindles more fire, pulling slabs of wood from a stack where restless mice shuffle in search of crumbs. He is leaving to forget his father in the bedroom, sleeping, before he wakes hungry for money or alcohol or violence, whichever comes first. He is leaving to forget his sisters in the washroom, scrubbing their hands raw against soapy dishes and rags — hermanas whom he knows will fall victim, daily, to his father's angers. He is leaving to forget, for now, his youngest brothers playing in the shadows of the sala, although he knows in a couple of years they too will join him in the US and follow his lead.

Like him, they will close the double entry door with wishes to return back to this place only after they strike rich in America. They will glance back once more at their mother standing in the corridor. Leaning on her good leg, my grandmother will hold onto the edges of her floral patterned apron, gathering handfuls of morning glories. In her fists she will carry a breath she does not release until they turn their back to her. When they leave to forget, the purple vines fly. She howls. Along the graveled road, they follow the seamlessly connected pink yellow blue green rows of adobe and brick houses lining the outskirts of town, move beside the rows of strawberry and potato fields where they once labored, stop to smell the mesquite trees that make the air thick and slow. It's a good year, each of them will note when they finally cross their father's milpa and look over the green sea of cornhusks dancing abundances they never profited from but saw, for a lifetime, stuffed in their father's pockets. They will leave to forget all of it, hopping into a truck driven by whichever eldest sibling is ready to take them to the border. Letting the dirt and dust explode and cloud under the tires of Rafa's red truck, my father looks back at a town he did not, until today, realize could look much smaller than it already was.

The way my mother tells it, when he finally crossed over into America, my father believed the world would not only expand for him, but that he too would be a larger man, more than his father and his father's milpa. Perhaps, for my father, the example of that man was an American. As a recent immigrant having little to no education and limited access to the English language, however, my father quickly learned the power white American men had over him. Because all of the men he worked under were white, and because when they were not white they talked white like my mother, he began to hunger for something that began to take on a shape similar to the one he had escaped but had no language for naming then.

Some of that hunger remained at bay when, about two years after having resided in Sacramento, California, my father met and fell in love with my mexicanamerican mother, whose native tongue was spanish and english.[1] Her tongue ran through the border, the irreducible mix already cutting her body's movement into the landscape she traversed, movement which never needed a boundary to exist in the first place. Never needed because her tongue, like the tongues of water, had been speaking; and never needed because, like el río running through the limit geographers mapped, she refused the dualism of the border that insisted she spoke two different languages. Instead, she swam

---

1   The phrase "whose native tongue was spanish and english" is inspired by lines from the chapter "Spanish is English" from Miriam Gurba's *Mean*: "I began as an only child with an only language. This language was English and Spanish." See Miriam Gurba, *Mean* (Minneapolis: Coffeehouse Press, 2017), 4.

in the plural beat of an unruly mouth that could never stand in one place long enough to see a binary. For she had been swept by a current that could imagine what nations could not: that she was something more splendid than two. My mother, having spent her life as a farmworker migrating between México and the United States, knew the power of language and knew how to pervert nationalistic ploys that used language as a means of violence. Because by the time my father met my mother she was a clerical worker, skilled typist, and writer (though she would never call herself one), she redistributed her privilege during her marriage with my father by helping him to apply for jobs and prepare for interviews until he landed a career as a cook. In an ideal world, my father would have felt solidarity with my mother who never used her literacy in English to make him feel inferior the way white men did. But my father still felt wounded and confused by a childhood tantrum he never cried to my grandfather.

Because my mother's English literacy troubled the gender hierarchies he was used to on both sides of la frontera, it didn't really matter whether my mother spoke English or Spanish: my father translated my mother's ability to speak English in this country as a threat to the manhood he never had validated on the other side of the border by his father but still sought validation from. In every *yeah* she responded to affirm him instead of *sí,* he saw himself shrink. In America, he was not supposed to feel small like he did in the stories of his childhood that he told my mother and that my mother translated and whispered to me in our secret language, which I thought was English until my father also learned how to speak it. Us two together telling his story, writing his life in unspoken colors he refused, my mother imagined me stories about that time, which was also many times, en aquellos tiempos, when my grandmother woke all of her children up at night to hide them in the nooks and crannies of the house, protecting them from whatever harm she would suffer when my grandfather came home after days and days of drinking. On most nights, María Elena managed to preserve her children from bearing witness to the beatings she would endure by guiding my drunken grandfather outside to where the livestock was, where her yells might have sounded more faint, where the neighbors could mistake her shrieks for the slaughtering of their pigs. But on the nights she was not able to guide my grandfather outside, the children must have caught glimpses in the crack of the door: pulled greñas and the hollowed out sound of two bodies thudding without (com)passion. And then there were times when my exhausted grandmother did not hear her husband come home and his hands reached her children, pulled them out of their slumber with boundless fists that took no shape in the dark. Some he dragged by the hair, some by the ears, kicking them outside of his adobe kingdom, out in the street, naked, with nothing but calzones as hard rain fell like nickels on their skin. If ever my grandfather came home drunk in the daylight, it was the men who suffered the beatings first. The women completing domestic labor inside the house, after hearing the sound of my grandfather abriendo el porton, had enough time to hide. After her daughters were safe, my grandmother would exit to the outdoor corridor in search of her battered sons. I can hear her endlessly pleading — ¡Ya párale, Luis! — a phrase that held mercy for me the one time my father gave me a belting in front of her.

Some of my tías read in between the silences, in the version of childhood horrors my tíos have spun for them, and theorize (chismeando) that my grandmother only ever became pregnant during nights like these. I read alongside the silences my tías leave open for more possibilities left in the cloaked nightmare of my father's childhood and imagine that perhaps my queerness extends itself across time to my grandfather, a man so broken by the men he longed to touch, a man who had been taught (chisme has it) by his traumatized Catholic mother to never touch himself, to never gift his body with pleasure, to never feel something deeper than shame, to pass that self-loathing to his sons and grandsons and, of course, his wife, my grandmother, whom he married through sexual shaming. Story has it my grandmother's parents were the wealthy Mexicans of the village, the more Spanish looking, and my grandfather saw marriage with my grandmother as a way out of his own poverty. After weeks of courting her through an aperture en una cerca that divided my great grandfather's land from the rest of the village, my grandfather reached across and touched my grandmother's hand. He left her with two choices: either marry him or he would tell her parents and everyone in the town that he had *touched* her and, therefore, ruined her. They married; and, although my grandmother was the eldest of her siblings, she inherited no money or property from her father because she was a woman. I am haunted by the touchless lives my grandmother and her children followed.

My grandfather, Luis, a father to my father Jose Luis, a once-upon-a-time son I am told was also once gentle, my father and my grandfather both longing to feel the other's touch, both fucked men reaching everywhere but toward the other, never learning, never loving, my father and grandfather abandoning the other, making men of each other, waiting for someone to fucking release them.

How much of my grandfather did I inherit as my father crossed the border, carried my grandmother in his flesh, and two years after meeting my mother, read my name aloud at my birth, just above my crying, or did he whisper it somewhere beneath my feet, only to hear the echo of his own name, and his father's name, burrowing its way underneath my skin. How much of the name escaped his teeth and left me holding a breath of a name so large between us he and I are still waiting to let go.

Longing to forget how powerless he had felt as both a victim and bystander of his father's patriarchal violence, my father promised nunca to my mother. He promised her *never* in Spanish, as if time could be promised without the past of his Mexican father or the future of white fathers in America. As if he could keep that word suspended in air, somewhere in the middle of the border, as if neither he nor men like Joaquín Murrieta had ever crossed it. He promised my mother never, which I now know translated to *forever*. My mother, her English language, her access to more opportunities, he read the way he did his father's out of reach pockets and, along with them, his father's unforgiving touch stinging heavy with the weight of hundreds of years and more. And like the many stories of Joaquín Murrieta I know, my father remembered his father when red crawled over my mother's skin, a map that once spread across my abuela nena's face sometime years before.

¡Ya párale, Jose Luis! ¡Ya párale Joaquín!

...

In the recurring nightmare,
the bullet is for me.
Sometimes, for my mother.
My narrow vision tells me
it is my turn
to let it enter
until there are no men behind the gun,
until the bullet cuts the air and
my flesh breathes —
bleeds.

I always have enough time to move but I don't.
I'm always too late.

When the bullet waits for my mother,
I'm still too late.

The sound of cockatiels wake me too soon.
Their flapping wings too late

and the wounded moans on time.

bird seeds scatter like pattering canicas
beside a mother
beside a song
white bars
below.

we try to pull the image apart
of a father
exposed
by words
he cannot yet say in English
so he musters up Spanish

soplando

while the bird flounders like fish

in between failing languages,
failing animals

my mother sings with birds,
her winged voice

planting translations,
seeds, not bullets,
into her sons.

...

This is how my body knows that the failed solidarity between men in my family begins with an earlier story of men failing women. This is how I know that there is an understory, in the undercurrents of my mother's tongue, underscoring the wounded sense of masculinity my father inherited as he waged war for life in America as having something to do with Joaquín's revolt and his failed alliance with other colonized people in John Rollin Ridge's text. What looks like failure between men begins with narratives of women who have been failed by men. But at the beginning of his novel, Ridge's Joaquín is self-reflexive enough to recognize that his Chicano rage against Anglos must also serve to liberate Chicanas. His bandit organization is only successful because Rosita, Carmelita, and Margarita fight armed and in masculine attire alongside the Chicanos. Additionally, before the women are excluded from Joaquín's plan, Joaquín draws his militant inspiration from the women who produce masculine and feminine Chicanx drag performances. When the bandits travel to Mokelumne Hill in Calaveras County, for example, nobody in the town suspects that the women would cause any harm because, "the women appeared in their proper attire, and were admired for their exceedingly modest and quiet deportment."[2] This is, of course, a part of their plan. At this juncture, Ridge intently emphasizes that the feminine garb operates as a genderqueer disguise for the benefit of the entire banditti. Because they blend in as "modest and quiet" women, the population of Mokelumne Hill does not suspect they are in any kind of real danger. They cannot fathom that what the women are rocking is a costume nor can they imagine that these women might be capable of violence. The novel posits a larger critique of this white heteronormative gaze following the banditti's movement at Mokelumne Hill when Harry Love, the man who will kill Joaquín at the narrative's end, enters their night camp ready to attack. After one of the women sounds a warning to notify the men of the intruders, the men are able to escape and the women go undetected once again because of their feminine costume:

> Upon entering, no one was to be seen but women, three of whom, then dressed in their proper garments, were the bandits' mistresses, of which fact, however, Love was ignorant. Leaving the women to shift for themselves, the fugitives went to their horses, which were hitched in an adjacent thicket, mounted them, and rode directly over to Oris Timbers, a distance of eight miles, where they immediately stole twenty head of horses and drove them off into the neighboring mountains. They remained concealed all the next day but at night came back (a movement wholly unanticipated by Love) to the cloth-house where they had left their women,

---

2   John Rollin Ridge, *The Life and Adventures of Joaquín Murieta* (New York: Penguin Classics, 1854), 27.

who quickly doffed their female attire and rode off with their companions into the hills, from which they had just come.[3]

Not only are the men saved by the perceptive woman who warns the entire camp of Love's presence, but Ridge's narrator emphasizes the women as wholly capable of holding the fort and defending themselves if ever a battle did ensue. Blinded by the "proper garments" that will be "doffed" off seconds after he is gone, Love fails in his mission.

Joaquín learns from the women that he can manipulate how white Anglo men racialize and gender his body. After he reads information on the Mexican bandit "character" newspapers and town gossip are after, Murrieta dresses up in so many elaborate costumes that he, according to our narrator, "was actually disguised the most when he showed his real features."[4] There is a queer undoing of patriarchal Chicano masculinity in Joaquín's tactical disguise following suit of the women who manipulate their gender not in wearing the men's clothes they prefer to wear throughout the novel but by dressing in the femme drag expected of them. Joaquín learns from the women how to refashion his image, how to escape the gaze of his pursuers by embodying different iterations of "Joaquín" and otherwise transgender masculinities that the women are also actively producing. While traveling Mokelumne Hill alongside the women, Ridge writes of Joaquín's most recent costume, "Joaquín *bore* the appearance and character of an elegant and successful gambler, being amply provided with means from his night excursions."[5] The word "bore" here is striking as it applies to Joaquín's "character," both in the sense of who he is but also in the sense of how the women teach him to write Chicano identity differently. We can read "bore" as ascribing, on the one hand, his bearing or carrying the appearance and character, like a letter on a page, he wants others to read, but also "bore" in its verb form, "to make hollow"

---

3   Ibid., 31.
4   Ibid., 27.
5   Ibid.

or "to make a hole in something" like the inside of a gun bar-rel, characterizes what the women do to Joaquín's masculinity.[6] His body, like the seemingly phallic gun barrel, is turned into an object that can not only shoot and penetrate but that can be entered, hollowed out, fucked, and read differently. The women, in this way, bore through channels of feminist possibilities that could liberate Joaquín from the violent patriarchal masculinity he encounters in California.

From the feminine sartorial performance, Murrieta learns how to put a hole into his "character" without a bullet, to blind the eyes of his pursuers by making himself porous and penetra-ble, vulnerable and malleable, untranslatable in language until he cannot be seen by a white gaze intent on killing him. Although we might read the women as refashioning their own woman-hood in the narrative, Joaquín's mirrored performance of the women suggests that these transgendering performances move beyond limited understandings of masculinity and instead work to liberate Chicanes from the grammar of white heterosexuality. To put it differently, the women *bore* through a limited lexicon that would only let Joaquín's Chicano performance arrive at leg-ible destruction and violence.

But despite the channel the women open for Joaquín's lib-eration, he does ultimately fail in solidarity with them, which he later recognizes. About halfway through the story, Joaquín declares himself the "head" of the entire movement and shifts away from collective Chicanx feminist rebellion. A paragraph after we read Joaquín's glorious speech, Margarita anticipates the danger in the revolt's new patriarchal structure and attempts to kill her abusive husband. Joaquín, who is sleeping in the same tent, catches Margarita with a knife in hand and orders at once that she drop it. In response, Margarita furiously throws the knife at Joaquín. Rather than address the internal community violence borne from the transition to the organization's patriar-chal order, Joaquín silences the issue. In challenging the organi-zation's sexism by resisting the hypermasculine turn Joaquín's

---

6   *Oxford English Dictionary,* s.v. "bore."

revolt takes, Margarita is cast as a traicionera and gets turned into a symbolic Malinche.

Based on the story of Malintzín, the Nahua woman who was sold into slavery and given to Hérnan Cortéz as a translator during the conquest, the myth of Malinche has been revised in the Chicanx imaginary to represent the Indian mother of mestizes as a race traitor because she both fucked with the colonizer's language and allegedly fucked the white man who conquered the Indigenous population in Mexico. The word *malinchista,* one my mother knew well out of her own mother's mouth for roughhousing with boys growing up and again for having had sex with my father when they eloped, is additionally used against Chicanas who defy Mexican heterosexual expectations of women. In this way, women who challenge Chicano authority, as Margarita does with Joaquín, are often read as having been corrupted by whiteness because they threaten Chicano patriarchy. Cherríe Moraga has drawn attention to how poet and writer Octavio Paz, in slandering Malinche with the title La Chingada (the fucked one), not only designated Malinche as a perpetually fucked subject, but used the myth as psychological warfare to portray women as violated victims who are also culpable for their own sexual victimization. In *The Labyrinth of Solitude* Paz builds off of Malinche's story to specifically assign unwavering positions between the chingón who "rips open the chingada" and the chingada "who is pure passivity." In response, Moraga details the traumatic experience of carrying the story of Malinche in the flesh as a Chicana lesbian by writing, "In the effort to avoid embodying la chingada, I became the chingón. In the effort to not feel fucked, I became the fucker, even with women. In the effort not to feel pain or desire, I grew callous around my heart and imagined I felt nothing at all."[7] The impact Malinche's myth has on Moraga's psyche reveals the ways in which the patriarchal narrative participates in inventing categorical divisions between masculinity and femininity as well as race and gender.

---

7   Cherríe Moraga, "A Long Line of Vendidas," in *Loving in the War Years,* 2nd edn. (Cambridge: South End Press, 2000), 115.

Gendered violence is produced by these artificial boundary lines, which mark the limit of the colonial imagination.

To think femininity and masculinity as indivisible, where the body producing masculinities is not a white cis man sectioned off and forbidden from producing femininities, would require a necessary disruption and departure from systems of domination that cannot conceive of a muscled tenderness and a tendered muscleness (for example) without assigning fixed racialized and gendered meanings to how we might possibly interact with, and touch, one another in language. Challenging the way Chicanos have translated Malinche's myth to produce narratives that position themselves closer to white men, as chingón fuckers, and Chicanas as chingada fucked "Indian" subjects, Chicanas reclaim the myth of La Malinche within a feminist context both for her symbolic defiance of Chicano patriarchy and for her insurgent betrayal of all the chingada/chingón binaries that keep us all from fully feeling present to ourselves and those whom we love and fuck with. For Joaquín to dismantle the system of white supremacy that pains him throughout Ridge's novel would necessitate that he take Margarita's lead, reposition himself in solidarity with her malinchidad, and join her in betraying the patriarchal structure of his own movement. In so doing, he would need to remember his own fuckedness, and learn how to re-read the beginning of his own story differently. He would need to, in other words, return to the source of his racial oppression and reframe the sense of his woundedness, which interprets Rosita's rape as the first injury directed at his own manhood. What would it mean for Joaquín to instead read Rosita's rape outside of the patriarchal paradigm that renders him a failed man and Rosita a ruined woman that needs his protection from becoming la chingada? It would, at the very least, mean liberating himself from the limiting position of el macho or el chingón by reclaiming Malinche's monstrous femininity. In so doing, he might thoroughly examine how his own sense of feeling like the white man's chingada is connected to Margarita's and Rosita's experiences with both white and Chicano patriarchies.

Notably, Joaquín does remove himself from toxic white masculinity and identifies the dangers of adopting the ways of white
men after one member of his band, Reis, abducts a white woman named Rosalie. While Reis and his men wander on a pleasure trip near the Stanislaus River, they spot a house and look in
through an illuminated window where Reis seems unsure as to
whether or not what he is witnessing is a scene of sexual violence or consensual loving. As he spots a man devouring Rosalie with kisses, Reis notes that "she could not restrain his wild
transports, for he caught her with a lover's fierceness around her
beautiful neck and breathed his soul upon her lips."[8] At times
Rosalie looks "bewildered" as she wrests herself out of this man's
embrace, which leaves Reis disturbed. Reis and his men enter
to rescue Rosalie and hold her captive. When days later Reis
tells Joaquín what he and his men have done, Joaquín scolds
Reis for torturing Rosalie and asks him whether he has raped
her. Reis says that he has done no such thing, to which Joaquín
reiterates that he too would never do such a thing, as he has
seen white men do to his partner Rosita and as he seen depicted
in the books Americans write. He scolds Reis, saying, "I ought
to kill you, but since you have had some honor and manhood
about you in this rascally matter, I will let you off this time."[9]
Joaquín critiques the misogynistic violence of white masculinity
while also affirming an older model of Spanish paternal masculinity he has inherited. After Rosalie thanks Joaquín for his
dignity in returning her home, Joaquín states, "yes, Señorita, I
am a man. I was once as noble a man as ever breathed, and if I
am not so now, it is because men would not allow me to be as I
wished."[10] Joaquín's mouth is teeming with transformative masculinities almost born into fruition. But his mouth falls short.
He recognizes that white men have not allowed him to be the
kind of man he was. He distinguishes himself in contrast their
misogyny and racism. But Joaquín does not tilt the axis of his

---

8   Ridge, *Joaquín Murieta*, 86.
9   Ibid., 91.
10 Ibid., 92.

world far enough to take an anti-patriarchal stance that would allow him to move alongside Chicanas like Margarita.

Although Joaquín fails to see the intersections between the racialized and gendered violences his band members experience, and despite his failure to understand racialized violence as also gendered, Margarita opens a path where readers of Ridge's novel might make the connection when she finally kills her husband and bores a channel through his body where his masculinity might be opened far enough to hold the pleasures, terrors, fears, pains, and joys of feeling vulnerable in the flesh. The killing happens a few days after Joaquín decides that only the men will leave into battle, while the women are left behind at Arroyo Cantua since, suddenly, the men believe it is no longer "prudent, in view of the bloody scenes which would be enacted, to take them along…."[11] While, for the first half of the novel, the women witness various bloody scenes, Joaquín's claim to leadership requires that the women be protected. The contradiction in the patriarchal reasoning could not be emphasized more when, three days after most of the men have left to go fight, Margarita is again brutally beaten by Guerra. The "bloody scene" the women should be preserved from is the one at home. Margarita takes matters into her own hands, and while everyone is asleep she pours a drop of hot lead, a bullet made liquid, in his ear with her "small and skillful" hand.[12] Because there is no sign of violence on his body the next morning, the men are confused as to how he died and conclude that he must have finally perished because of his alcoholism. Margarita cries the entire next day but her tears are not remorseful, says our narrator, since soon after Guerra's death she accepts Isadora Conejo — whose name is feminine — as her next husband, and they both live happily ever after. Ridge's narrator instructs us to read Guerra's death and Margarita's tears and subsequent joy through the following verse written by Lord Byron: "Woman's tears, produced at will,

11   Ibid., 70.
12   Ibid., 71.

/ Deceive in life, unman in death."[13] The excerpt suggests that Margarita's tears deceive, not because her pain is not real but because rather than mourn the loss of Guerra she mourns the kind of life Guerra never lived. Like the bullet lead she turns to liquid, her tears perform an unmanning of Guerra, a softening and liquifying of his body to indistinguishable masculine and feminine synergies so that his corpse can explore liberation and life beyond the language of war and femicide that produced his body and name. Boring through his ear, Margarita also helps us readers hear previously inaudible sonic pathways we have yet to articulate in language, our mouths left wide open with a silent wish.

---

13   Ibid.

2

Joaquín As Myself

Because I have survived the story of Joaquín, the bullet of my father, out of my mother's skilled mouth and as my mother's son, I ran from my father and looked to understand not the power he or my abuelo had over femeninos like me or chingona women like my mother, for that seemed quite insignificant and uninteresting to me, but what the historical power of my mother's shape-shifting language did to my father's distorted masculine psyche. I had, for a long time, naively assumed that her secret power inhered in her ability to speak English and, because I spoke English like my mother, I believed I had escaped my father's wounded sense of masculinity. But that was when I had thought that the wound was only just a story with one beginning and one end — when I had thought the wound was just my immigrant father living Joaquín's life, when I had thought that there was just one border to cross, one father to raise me. When I began attending Cosumnes River College, as a first-generation college student at the age of 18, I began to sense how this ongoing history of border-crossing and the encounter with patriarchy held me hostage. I had by the time I enrolled in college decided I was going to become a writer and study the language I believed my mother used to paint me stories, which at the time I still believed was called English. But the language I studied in English Writing and Literature courses, like the language I had studied in all of my K-12 schooling, fell short of my mother's telling: her transitional movement between spanishes and englishes, sounds that slipped in the music between her words, phrases she turned over into images of light and feeling, weighted color that activated my vision to azules profundos-verdes ligeros-moradas pesadas, colors that could dig into her long stretched pauses that left her eyes closed conjuring spatial fields I could travel once she spoke, her mouth and eyes collapsing into one vessel.

...

The first essay I ever wrote for school, I wrote with you.
Your quiet
blared
alongside me as your damp dark
hair lighted
rain
into the calm of the night

Together, we read my fifth grade teacher's prompt:
"Write a biography about someone important to your life."

Important to my life
also meant important to you
So I chose your sister
The one who lived to seventeen
by catching up to a breath not her own
The one whose heart had a passage
missing.
In words,
we tried to make it —
the pulse of her life
the same year Selena died.
I wrote the essay when I was ten.
I only had enough oxygen to remember Veronica for three.

I wrote the best I could
Remembering on torn wrinkled scratch paper
commaless fragments
drawing the outline of a sister.
You remembered deeper
with me
Typing,
marking the page with our voices,
answering questions to memories that were not mine.

The next day my teacher read my writing.
He knew it wasn't mine.
I told him it wasn't.
He didn't understand
how you left room for my memory to catch up
to something you and I could share
with the dead.
Letters he did not know,
he had forgotten
that this remembering was what writing looked like.

I thought that Mr. Valdivia would have been upset the day he asked me if I wrote my 5th grade project all by myself. In fact, I feared the discipline and punishment I would suffer. So I lied to him. But he insisted that I could not have written it on my own since I was recalling memories of my tía Veronica that I had not been alive to witness. I gave in and admitted that my mother had helped me reconstruct her sister's heart with me in writing. To my surprise, he responded, "How wonderful it must be to have a mother to write with." Mr. Valdivia was the first Chicano English teacher I ever had and it was in his words I saw that what separated our experience surviving English classrooms was generational privilege. He never had a mother to write with. He identified with me, but also longed for the kind of authorship my mother and I had created. In so doing, he betrayed student codes of conduct and his training in handling student plagiarism. Instead, he made a conscious choice to affirm the idea that writing was a collaborative rather than individual process I should continue pursuing with my mother.

I am forever dreaming my way back to her language, extending beyond my fingertips.

...

As a migrant, my mother knew how to make words move. For most of my life, I moved with the improvisation of her language; but, the longer I stayed in school while completing my undergraduate and graduate degrees, I felt in me a desire stir that pulled me further and further away from my mother's movement and, strangely, no, deceivingly, closer and closer to the choreography of my father's life. When I attended college, I did not learn how to write or how to tell stories from the worlds I came from. Rather, I had entered a space where the study of English meant I was going to learn how to closely read and study white fathers. Didn't I, after all, begin my first college essay with a quote by Ralph Waldo Emerson? Didn't I, in the same paper, feel inspired by Gloria Anzaldúa (who I first read in the same college composition course) to write an essay about my own multilingualism not in the wildly free unapologetic feminist language of her book *Borderlands/La Frontera* but in the sterile unwavering language of academia? In those first years of my college education, where I not only learned proper MLA format and how to organize my essays with logical coherent arguments my professors could understand, and where I also learned about aquel Emerson, y ese Mark Twain, y el otro Walt Whitman in American Literature courses, I began to feel, for the first time in my life, larger than my father because it was the closest I would ever get to looking like a middle-class white man. This was a dangerous feeling. I was, in other words, fulfilling my father's own lifelong unrealizable dream, the unreachable promise of patriarchy. My sudden access and entry into white spaces meant

I was suddenly closer to the patriarchal power my father would never know in the US and yet still desired.

...

How can I tell you now, páp, that after all these years of studying, I who have acquired some of this power, have moved closer to it, that I have learned it is not something to desire? You who have wanted this so long for yourself, how can I tell you that I'm trying to betray all of my training as your son and as theirs? How can I tell you that I'm working my way out of a mouth that was never mine? Como te puedo decir que escribo, I write, as an attempt to open space for us to move and imagine being free? Como te puedo decir que nos robaron de nosotros? It's kept you from you, kept me from me, kept us from us? Como te puedo decir sin decirte que I thought I could be free one day if I only learned to write like them. Then, they would finally see me. Then, I would belong in this country. Even while writing this, I see the limits — I, a trained academic — the ways I restrain my voice from coming out to say what I want to say. Que nos queremos. I did not yet imagine that behind the pages of my writing was not a white man but my ancestors, my mother, my father, my sisters, my brothers, my students: the sum of me carrying me on the other side, waiting, and unafraid. I did not yet know how many words I had that white professors could not read and that I never really intended for them to read. I did not see the words I still do not know, will never utter, but feel resounding in strained melodious chants, the honeyed texture of our belonging.

...

I see it more clearly now: me stepping foot on campus at the age of eighteen to study English Literature, the campus where I would eventually come back to work as an English Professor, while my father worked and continues to work as a cook in the cafeteria at American River College, the sister campus to the community college I had first attended. My entry into the college classroom marked a border crossing over into the white middle class I believed had finally set me free of my father's history and the men like him. The institutionalized literacy that produced me as a scholar, however, did not take me out of my father's wound but reproduced it. Placed me neatly in its web of historical violence, pulled me towards my father even as it ripped me from his flesh. It is in the classroom that I was in training — as a student, and again one day as a professor — to learn and adopt, and to be an agent of the white heteropatriarchal ideologies that wounded my father and, before him, that mysterious looming figure some called Joaquín.

In my lifetime, I have been increasingly incorporated into an institutional structure informed by legacies of white colonization and patriarchal dominance in the US that have also kept my communities on the margins, working where my father worked. The geography of the border is housed in the space of the university. First-generation college students who make it into college English classrooms are exposed to a rhetoric of racial, gender, and class dominance that still tell them their communities do not belong there. We are taught to evaluate ourselves and our successes through the language of white conquest. It is from professors that I learned to *master* the standard English language by using *appropriate* language (what I heard was *be straight*), by writing in *error-free* prose (what I heard was *don't speak so Mexican*), and by becoming a *self-reliant* evaluative reader and writer (what I heard was *be like Ralph Waldo Emerson*). These learning objectives, which I saw outlined in countless syllabi my professors handed out, had consequences outside of the institution and deeply informed how I began choreographing myself in relation to my communities.

They also had an effect in training us students of color, if we became professors and teachers one day, to have mastery over the students of color we would train to look more like us, which really just meant to look as close as they could get to looking like a white scholar. I remember when I first became a full-time English faculty member at my college, I was disappointed in the failed solidarity I witnessed among faculty of color who remained committed to institutionalized forms of English literacy and grammar that perpetuated harm on our Black and Brown students. As a recent hire, I had hoped to bind to my colleagues of color and that, together, we would incite revolt against the cis white heteropatriarchal supremacist structures of the English classroom and the entire college. But I was met by some faculty who had been so harmed by the university and their own experiences in graduate school that they practiced harming other students and faculty members. Bruised they bruised. Oppressed they oppressed. Colonized they colonized. Straddling their position of power as professors and their position as marginalized people, they were engaged in reproducing the very same trauma that harmed them. To teach our students to read and write was to prepare them for war. Didn't they, after all, have to work a million times harder at performing white respectability than the white colleagues in my department to get where they were? To understand them, I had to recognize eventually that what I was experiencing was not unique to the college I worked at, but that the structure of every university depends on faculty of color dominating one another in their commitment to academic literacy. To survive as faculty, we are taught to survive the same way we survived our instruction as students; isolated and removed from our communities in this white space, we move in a world of grammar afraid to return home and speak to the bodies that should be family in classrooms and departments.

It was in my first year of teaching as a full-time professor, as I also taught John Rollin Ridge's novel, that I recognized how the structure of the university that had kept my community out was not going to change simply because I was now in it. My success in the university, instead, was determined by how well I conformed to whiteness; and it is within that structure that there was always the temptation to dominate my own Mexican father. I was, to put it differently, to continue my father's desire to dominate his father even as I believed I was resisting that desire by studying the language he could not read or write.

...

When, after years of *escaping* the story of my father by studying Literature, becoming a literary scholar and professor of English, I finally read John Rollin Ridge's version of the myth of Joaquín, I began to see where I — as a reader and writer trained in the English language — stood in the architecture of this ongoing tale. And the wound was in the language I spoke. And I too was Joaquín, opening my mouth climbing out of the story anew.

Given its foundational place in American Literature, Ridge's text reveals a lot to me about the pinched psychological landscape Ridge must have inhabited as a Cherokee writer detailing the plight of the legendary Mexican bandit in English to a limited Anglo-American audience. The story itself seems to serve as a psychic mirror, wherein the white reader should finally see the costs of failing to incorporate a noble Mexican man into the nation. They should, in other words, see that Joaquín's violent banditry was produced by American racism. They should see that Joaquín died because they made him. But in the mirror Ridge produces, I also see the bent shape of my imagination asking: How much of the white reader do I see reflected back at me, generations away from when Ridge wrote the text, as I read a book my Mexican father cannot? If we remember Ridge not only as a writer but as a *reader* of Joaquín's life, we see him struggling in the text with this very question. Reflected not only in Ridge's choice to pen *The Life and Adventures of Joaquín Murieta* under the translation of his Cherokee name, Yellow-Bird, but also the book's title, wherein he anglicized Murrieta's Spanish last name by dropping the double rolling *rr,* is a story about Ridge's conflicted and pained investment in English literacy. Ridge's version of Joaquín's life stresses, following in the tradition of the corrido, that the legendary bandit could read and write well in English.

...

And so it begins again, before Ridge tells the story, in the corrido of *Joaquín Murrieta,*

> Yo no soy Americano
> pero comprendo el inglés
> Yo lo aprendí con mi hermano
> al derecho y al revés
> A cualquier americano
> lo hago temblar a mis pies
>
> Cuando apenas era un niño
> huérfano a mí me dejaron.
> Nadie me hizo ni un cariño,
> a mi hermano lo mataron
> Y a mi esposa Carmelita,
> cobardes la asesinaron…
>
> I am not American
> but English I understand
> I learned it with my brother
> forwards and backwards
> I make any Anglo tremble at my feet
>
> When I was barely a child
> I was left an orphan.
> No one gave me a bit of affection,
> They killed my brother,
> and some cowards
> Killed my wife Carmelita[1]

The most known and popularized version of the corrido was recorded in 1934 by Los Madrugadores. The lyrics I cite above are pulled from that version. Despite the recording, however, the corrido itself has neither a recognizable individual author

---

[1]   Los Madrugadores, "Joaquín Murrieta," 1934.

we can locate and no fixed origin point in time.[2] And so as the lyrical myth of an untraceable mouth would have it, it's not just Joaquín's capacity for violence that terrifies Anglo-Americans, it is primarily that he and his brother are bilingual. That his brother has taken the language from its colonial institutionalized setting and that he has redistributed his alphabetical knowledge in kinship, points to an otherwise deviant use of language, something akin to the way my mother used it with me. By learning English *al derecho y al réves,* his brother runs the alphabet, teaches him to make language move like the poetics of the corrido that disrupt the teleological only forward moving empire hostile to their bodies. This is not to say that their shared language spoken in kinship, however, transcends the colonial wound of either standardized Spanish or English. As my friend José Arellano has suggested to me in our discussion of the corrido, the murder of Joaquín's brother is also, symbolically, a theft of the source of his learning English, similar to the theft I felt the university made of my mother's language. But while the death of Joaquín's brother repeats and dramatizes the colonial violence of imposed English and enforced Anglo patriarchal nationalism on Mexicans, there is still, perhaps, if we move forwards and backwards to a third point in time, another temporary theft enacted by Joaquín and his brother, my mother and I, that remains unrecognizable to the state and unlocatable even within the enclosed space of the nation and grammatical English. As the song relays the history of Joaquín learning English in a Spanish song, the hierarchical relationship and categorical distinction between English and Spanish, and the written and oral word, collapses. The supposed purity of written English is thrown into crisis by the plurilingual voice telling the story, tampering and ruining every language ever uttered and sung not before colonization but in the corrido(r) of an open wound.

---

2   See Luis Leal, "El Corrido de Joaquín Murrieta: Origen y Difusión," *Mexican Studies/Estudios Mexicanos* 11, no. 1 (1995): 1–23, and Shelly Streeby, *American Sensations: Class, Empire, and the Production of Popular Culture* (Berkeley: University of California Press, 2002), 275.

...

Building on the corrido, Ridge's Joaquín dramatizes Joaquín's fluid literacy most when Joaquín descends into the city of Stockton like a bisexual bilingual god. As the men and women of the town flirt on the corners of the streets, a mysterious "fine-looking" figure disruptively attracts the attention of the men and women alike and "without seeming to know it, he [is] observed by all observers."[3] Because Joaquín is not wearing a disguise as he usually does, his "real features" function as a costume and so the townspeople do not recognize the man they all desire as the murderous bandit they have seen. As Murrieta stops to read a series of notes posted on a nearby house, everybody continues drooling over him. Among the scraps of paper he finds are job announcements, items for sale, and rewards for his capture. Nearly all of the posts are written imperfectly: "for sale" is, for example, spelled "For SAIL"; "notice" is marked down as "notis"; "offer" is rendered "offur."[4] Joaquín proves he can read and write better than any of the poor and working-class Anglos of Stockton by responding to the reward for his own capture. Taking out his pencil, he marks down in perfect spanglish, "I will give $10,000. Joaquín."[5] The people of Stockton are speechless and "nothing else was talked of for a week."[6] Their inability to speak of anything else other than the bandit's literacy amplifies the hierarchical relationship between the written and oral word, where Joaquín's inscription rises above the town's voices below the mountain. His decision to write his Spanish name con accento, however, also disrupts that hierarchy by sitting alongside the "white trash" misspellings on the wall that also work against the rules of standardized English. My friend Emma reads the misspelling of the word "sail," for example, as a possible challenge to the boundaries that secure white property through

3 John Rollin Ridge, *The Life and Adventures of Joaquín Murieta* (New York: Penguin Classics, 1854), 58.

4 Ibid., 58–59.

5 Ibid., 59.

6 Ibid.

economies of Mexican death. Like the word "sale," taken out of
its contextual relationship to property and redirected in relation
to a "sail" associated with water and fluidity, Joaquín's name dis-
turbs the pattern of English grammar on the page that treats his
dead body as us property.[7] By writing his name in Spanish on
a document he isn't supposed to read, he uses language within
a plurilanguaging Chicanx tradition even as his knowledge of
refined English also places him intimately near the Anglo men
who want him dead for reward. His teetering ascension and de-
scension through English fluency paints an unsettling picture of
his fluctuating position in nineteenth-century California.

In the world of the text, Joaquín is the tragic mestizo. The
pain of his life is that even in his position as a well-read Mexican with the white skin of a Spaniard that is "neither very dark
or very light, but clear and brilliant," he is not granted full citizenship nor is he completely spared from anti-Mexican racism.[8]
After the Mexican–American war ended with the signing of
the Treaty of Guadalupe Hidalgo, Article 9 of the treaty allowed
Mexicans already living in annexed us territories to remain
and enjoy "all the rights of the citizens of the United States" as
long as they did not "preserve the character of citizens of the
Mexican Republic."[9] Joaquín's decision to write his "character"
on the bounty claim is a clap back to the grammar of the law
that insists he relinquish any sign of his Mexicanness and assimilate into whiteness. The effects of the treaty made it so all
white and mestizo Mexican/Latino men, since the law only tan-
gentially secured the rights of men, found themselves categori-
cally made a non-white, non-Caucasian, people of color whose
rights to own property in us territories were questionable un-
less they assimilated. Following the establishment of the border,
California passed a series of additional laws that would define
the parameters of whiteness through the invention of Anglo-

---

7 Ibid.
8 Ridge, *Joaquín Murieta*, 8.
9 "Treaty of Guadalupe Hidalgo (1848)," *National Archives*, https://www.
   archives.gov/milestone-documents/treaty-of-guadalupe-hidalgo.

Americanness. In 1851, for example, California instantiated the Foreign Miner's Tax Law, which was supposed to enforce taxes on foreign-born miners who wanted to mine for gold. In practice, however, the tax was mostly applied to Mexican and Chinese people after the law modified "foreign-born" to exclude "free white persons" who could potentially become American citizens one day.[10] After various uprisings and attacks led by Indigenous, Californian, Mexican, and Latinx people were aimed at Anglos in response to Indigenous and Mexican removals, the state passed the Anti-Vagrancy Act in 1855, also known as the "Greaser" Act, which legalized the arrest of any people with Spanish *or* Indian blood who might not be "peaceable or quiet persons."[11] By nearly equating "Spanish" and "Indian" blood, "Spanish" like "Mexican" came to designate all Latinx people (Chilean, Argentinian, Peruvian etc.) in California as a miscegenated race deemed inferior to the Anglo race due to their possible Indigenous mestizaje. Laws against vagrancy not only shaped the white American imaginary in California by conflating Latinx and Indigenous differences into the singular image of the criminal "Mexican" immigrant but also created the conditions for extralegal lynchings to which hundreds of "Mexicans" fell victim.[12] The response to these colonial traumas for many white and light-skinned mestizes was, of course, to relinquish themselves of their newly invented racial character in the US as best they could by denying their Indigenous, African, and afromestize cultural heritage, by learning English, and by practicing racism against — and distancing themselves from — their Chinese, Black, and Indigenous relations. Through Joaquín's fluid racial position as a white Mexican, Ridge choreographs the vigi-

---

10 Jean Pfaelzer, *Driven Out: The Forgotten War against Chinese Americans* (Berkeley: University of California Press, 2007), 20–24.

11 Robert F. Heizer and Alan J. Almquist, *The Other Californians: Prejudice and Discrimination under Spain, Mexico, and the United States to 1920* (Berkeley: University of California Press, 1977), 151.

12 Ken Gonzales-Day, *Lynching in the West: 1850-1935* (Durham: Duke University Press, 2006).

lante's right to citizenship according to the fractures of white-ness that drew nineteenth century color lines in California.

In the novel, we see Ridge incorporate Joaquín into Califor-nia through complex and irresolvable raciolinguistic terms.[13] Joaquín's literacy is a power move. By representing Murrieta as a writer of English, Ridge renders him more worthy of citizen-ship to his white Anglo readers than the illiterate white Anglo populations in Stockton. This move is strategic and confusing. The entire book is framed by foregrounding Murrieta's educa-tion and respectable upbringing which leads Ridge to write some splintering conclusions implying that those who cannot read like Joaquín are not only more susceptible to racism but also far less American than him:

> The country was then full of lawless and desperate men, who bore the name of Americans but failed to support the hon-or and dignity of that title. A feeling was prevalent among this class of contempt for any and all Mexicans, whom they looked upon as no better than conquered subjects of the United States, having no rights which could stand before a haughtier and superior race. They made no exceptions. If the proud blood of the Castilians mounted to the cheek of a partial descendant of the Mexiques, showing that he had inherited the old chivalrous spirit of Spanish ancestry, they looked it as a sausy presumption in one so inferior to them. The prejudice of color, the antipathy of races, *which are al-ways stronger and bitterer with the ignorant and unlettered,* they could not overcome, or if they could, would not, be-cause it afforded them a convenient excuse for their unmanly cruelty and oppression.[14]

---

13 For a more extensive analysis of the term "raciolinguistic," see Nelson Flores and Jonathan Rosa, "Undoing Appropriateness: Raciolinguistic Ideologies and Language Diversity in Education," *Harvard Educational Re-view* 85, no. 2 (2015): 149–71, and Jonathan Rosa, *Looking Like a Language, Sounding Like a Race* (New York: Oxford University Press, 2019).

14 Ridge, *Joaquín Murieta,* 9.

Despite the periods that divide Ridge's multiple claims, they, like an ouroboros, consume themselves before the reader can pause and swallow each sentence. In the process of claiming citizenship for Murrieta as a "lettered" subject, Ridge draws class distinctions that contradict the social order of Anglo whiteness in the us because Murrieta is situationally closer to it through his English fluency than poor and working-class white Anglos. The logic of the passage above goes: those who can read Ridge's novel should distance themselves from the allegedly racist attitudes of the uneducated Anglos, those who cannot read should learn to overcome their ignorant racism by learning how to read, and those who continue to practice racism are *unmanly* and unrefined Americans. Ridge's critique of whiteness as "a convenient excuse for cruelty" unlettered whites capitalize on is an attempt to get elite whites to think themselves above practicing racism against Chicanes like Joaquín. But to make that claim Ridge invests in institutionalized English fluency that, in the us, lives in the domain of the *manly* noble white literati who can, like Ridge and his Murrieta, read his book. And that investment produces in Joaquín a patriarchal Chicano masculinity that also reproduces the scene of failed solidarity among the colonized. By placing Murrieta in closer proximity to his honorable Anglo readers, he sets him apart not only from poor whites but also from the illiterate Mexican, Chinese, and Indigenous populations in the text.

It is worth noting, however, that within the circle of the Mexican community, Ridge depicts Joaquín as seemingly aware and eerily uneasy about his relationship to whiteness. Ridge writes,

Joaquín knew his advantages. His superior intelligence and education gave him the respect of his comrades, and, appealing to the prejudice against the "Yankees," which the disastrous results of the Mexican war had not tended to lessen in their minds, he soon assembled around him a powerful band

of his countrymen, who daily increased, as he ran his career
of almost magical success.[15]

It is unclear whether or not Joaquín actually thinks of himself
as "superior" because of his education or if he knows he will
be perceived as such by his community. It is also unclear as to
whether the educational "advantages" describe the power he
has over his community, or if his advantages are those he has
over Anglos who cannot anticipate that among the Mexican
bandits is someone who can not only read in English but who
can redistribute that unevenly distributed knowledge and power
to the masses. What Joaquín seems to know is that what binds
Mexicans together is their common hatred for the "Yankees,"
but that also caught up in that hatred is his tongue, and Ridge's,
who, because they can speak like them, remain tongue tied, in
a forever war with themselves and the histories that produced
the institutionalized setting of the English classroom in the us.

...

The way I remember it, I always heard your red Ford F-150
truck before I saw you pick me up from school. Corridos — ran-
cheras — cumbias — norteñas — banda — mariachi blasted out
of your windows. It was this music that had made me want
to wear your chaleco, the one that boasted MICHOACÁN on
the back. The one with the fringes. You have always been a bad
dancer, but I loved how the threads swayed with you and the
music, especially when you danced a cumbia with mom, and I
wanted to look as pretty as you did dancing to the sounds the
kids at school could not distinguish and would only recognize
as "Mexican" music.

They didn't know how we moved in the music. They didn't
know it was the only time my body felt truly free to move next
to yours. They didn't know the evenings after school, when orange and pink blanketed the Sacramento sky, how mis herma-

---

15 Ridge, *Joaquín Murieta*, 14.

nos y yo tomábamos tiempo, stole time away from practicing our spelling, to dance with you and mom as you played Chente's *La Ley del Monte* on loop from your boom box in the living room... *Grabé en la penca un magüey tu nombre/unido al mío, entrelezados...* The song would tell the story, again and again, of two young lovers who, on a maguey leaf, inscribed their names years ago to declare their love for one another before they were separated by unfortunate and unclear circumstances. After having been away for so long, when the singer (Vicente Fernández) returns to his hometown to find that his lover has made a life with another, he is heartbroken. He rebukes his lover for not waiting for him and for forgetting the history of the love they had once documented. It was the lover, he reminds them, who chose the prettiest maguey in town and suggested that he record, along with the intertwined initials he had grooved into the leaf, two tangled hearts with an arrow piercing through. Vicente responds to the lover — who claims that the story he is telling is not true and only made up words — by urging the lover to listen to the maguey because the stalks still speak. Although the leaf has since been cut since the night you exchanged my love for someone else's, he says, and although you cut the stalk that reminds you of me, if you only looked through my eyes you too would see the new leaves that sprout, que brotan, marked with our names.

What I think Vicente means when he says the maguey still remembers is that the water stored inside the thick membranes of its leaves holds the memory. Even if the lover cuts la penca off, the water held throughout its entire body remembers what it was connected to and what had been written on its forgotten limb years ago. The newborn leaves that sprout from that place carry those markings, hidden deep within the water's flesh. The song reminds me how you and I are linked by name. When I first learned to write my name. I was in kindergarten attending bilingual school. I was writing it in English and Spanish then. It was the first time I realized I could spell myself anew. It was the first time I felt I could keep remaking myself. Deliberately, I omitted "Luis" from my full name even when my teacher reminded me to put down Jose ~~Luis~~ on the wide ruled sheets we were using in class. There was so much room left to write you next to me, but even then, I knew that I wanted to tear myself away from that part of you I had no language for. I wanted to chop off a part of you I was inheriting the way Vicente's lover tore la penca to forget the love and pain they shared. I felt that by excising my grandfather's name, standing in the middle of us, that I was cutting off the part I didn't want to inherit. Because that name, Luis, I had only ever heard when my mother was in despair and called you by your full name, Jose Luis, or when my grandmother, with the echo of her husband, also said your name in a tone I feared. And so I stopped spelling myself in your shadow at school, thinking it was very easy to free myself of our shared history.

And then I began to spell my name in English. It was the year I was in the fourth grade that I learned to feel ashamed of your music and my body. It was my first year in an English Only! classroom. It was the year I learned language could be reduced to one color. It was the year of 9/11 when I learned that the color of my language was brown. It was the year my brother Sergio, el más moreno de mis hermanos, was a "Middle Eastern," an "Indian," a "Mexican," and a "terrorist" all at once. And so I began to loathe my name because the mouths that spoke at school rejected the Mexican in me but also because I had already started to reject you because you both feared and rejected the vieja in me.

…

I am your vieja / stolen by my mother's movement / I anticipate your weapon like we're playing Lotería / la escoba / you ask me to sweep / You have never taught me how / I've already lost your game / I dance with the broom / cock my hip / launch myself into each tile / Maná, or Selena, or Prince, or Otis, or Juan Gabriel / my mother's music / breaks the ground open / I hold the broom to write a story / the way my mother does / her feet jump along the cream grid / pause / dance / my chin her chin atop the broom / my head her head slanted to the side / my eyes her eyes flooding the living room with primrose / a memory of an arroyo / arrests her / shocks me into motion / the water before the houses were built along the bank of Jalostotitlan / the water that hid the devil / mis abuelos warned her / no seas coqueta con el diablo / I flirt with the broom / the pinesoled floor is marked with the residue of my mother's footprints / You do not strike me / you take the broom / you teach me how to spell myself in your name

...

Back then I still believed that school was a refuge away from you, but my hatred for you and my culture merged from feeling unsafe in my body both at home and at school. I imagine, as I climb in your loud red truck, white children giggling at us. I crouch. Hide below the backseat window, hoping nobody will know that the man drowning out their imaginary laughter is my father... *Grabé en la penca un magüey tu nombre/unido al mío, entrelezados...* playing a song that remembers our dancing names.

...

At the edge of Ridge's writing I hear in my voice, a long-ago cry across time saying en inglés too pale, *I talk just like you. I'm not like my Mexican father.* A pained cry echoes. The sound sinks, vibrating its way into the familiar violence my English education in the US continues to pose in my life. I learned to read, I learned to write, I opened books, and, cowering away from mi cultura, mis lenguas, wrote letters to the white man even when my teachers and professors did not look like white men. It was in school that I learned how those letters could be used against you.

Do you remember páp? Do you remember I put all the white learning into practice by making my sudden access to power over you known? I was preparing to transfer to San Francisco

State University. Softening yourself onto the sofa, the worn-out springs groaned underneath us as you, for the first time since I had received my acceptance letters to four-year colleges, sat beside me to talk about my future. You didn't congratulate me because you felt threatened by my education and my leaving your dominion. You couldn't offer me money because we didn't have it and, probably, because by then your gambling addiction had worsened. So you offered me family, telling me to make sure to connect with my prima Rosa, your goddaughter, who was studying at SFSU to become a nurse. Rosa was not only a first-generation college student, like me, but had also migrated to the US when she was 18. She and her friend circle reflected her commitment to Mexican and Latinx culture in ways I envied but did not admit to you. Instead, I replied to your offer by saying words I knew could cut you open. Con corazón frío, I said I did not want to connect with her because all her friends were *pai-sas. Like you,* is what I meant to follow with but I said it without saying it. I weaponized the word *paisa* to see you speechless, to leave you without language. I said it because for once in my life I wanted you to know where I stood, which was nowhere near you, which I didn't know was also so damn close to you and your pain. My mouthful of words, your silence, two emotional bruises merging. Both of us failing our mothers. Me failing my chingona paisa prima, who would eventually come to save me in friendship and teach me how to practice my own paisaness y jotería.

I didn't see how wrong I was because I did not want to see it. Your pain. Because I did not want to see that you were trapped, that I was trapped. I did not want to ask you if you were hurt, if you had been hurting for a long time, both from the pain of the masculinity handed down to you and from the words you did not have. I also did not know what I would look like without my anger for you. I refused to see you fully, because I was afraid that to recognize your pain of living as a paisa in this country might somehow take away from my pain living as both a paisa's son and a maricón. I thought it would discount how my brothers and I are still healing from your femmephobia and homophobia. I thought it would take away from my mother's pain, that my admitting that she did have power in this country as an English literate pocha with white privilege, would somehow take away from her experiences of migrating between two countries and laboring in the fields of Winters, Dixon, Davis, and West Sacramento at the age of fourteen. I thought that it would erase what I knew about her suffering under the Mexican Catholic patriarchal order of her father and her sudden transition into yours. Recognizing your pain, I felt, would round you out so much as a character in the life story I kept telling myself, that I would then have to be the villain instead of you.

...

But the thing about dismantling patriarchy is that it requires that we stumble into the story we do not want to tell, which is often the story of our own indoctrination into patriarchy. And I have been afraid to remember how when my mother told me to "be un hombresito" sometimes she meant "be responsible, be kind," while at other times she meant, "do what your father says," because she could not protect me. I suppose the resistance to tell that story comes from a fear that uncovering our woundedness is an ongoing process, a painful task that really has no end. And I have been afraid to examine my own proximity to patriarchy and the ways in which, because my brownness is situational in this country, I am in even closer proximity to inhabiting the role of the patriarch in the US than my father is. So I'm trying to understand fully how I have access to this patriarchy, in part, because my mother also had access to it, while I am also revisiting how my father deployed gender dominance and domestic violence as a colonized man of color who lived within the walls of my childhood house.

It has taken me years to stop running from that house, and even more years to stop running from the historical forces that have given shape to my life. In *The Will to Change: Men, Masculinity, and Love* the Black feminist pedagogue and writer bell hooks helps me understand myself and my relationship to the past a little better when she talks about how men hurt by their fathers often narrativize their lives by promising to live a life in opposition to how their fathers lived. Referring to a teachable moment where the men in her classroom confess that because they often have no model for love between fathers and sons, they often think of the opposite of what their fathers would do, hooks responds and writes to us,

> I affirm this practice, adding that it is not enough to stay in the space of reaction, that being simply reactive is always to risk allowing that shadowy past to overtake the present. How many sons fleeing the examples of their fathers raise boys who emerge as clones of their grandfathers, boys who may never even have met their grandfathers but behave just like them?[16]

For hooks, dismantling patriarchy requires that we move beyond claiming an antagonistic relationship to our fathers and that we instead analyze how patriarchy works as an assault by gendering our bodies across nonlinear time. To vision other forms of love and masculinity, we must do work on the shadowy pasts we do not, and will never, have complete access to. Children who carry transgenerational trauma often become good readers of our parents' shadows. We learn to access them by becoming students of their silence, and we engage a lifetime of studying what is not said because we learn early on that silence has a sound and a depth that cannot be locked down but that is nonetheless there. We learn that silence is not nothing. That it tells a story. Although I might never fully know the layers of erasure that continue to produce the same kind of men in my family, I am committed to read the conflicted shadows of patriarchal colonizations colliding in me and in the language I speak and write from. What this means is that I want to write in the practice of unknowing my past, to speculate across time and

---

16 bell hooks, *The Will to Change: Men, Masculinity, Love* (New York: Washington Square Press, 2004).

space and see the multiple ways I can exist and speak beyond the patriarchal ordering I was born into. I want to live in the form of questions that seek no answer.

...

Questions I was never trained to ask my grandmother nena about my grandfather: If he desired or envied, desired and envied, her wealthy Spanish father, the one the village called El Guero. What life was like for my darker-skinned grandfather living in the campos of Atecucario. If what she told my mother, *that the blessing of having all boys was muchos cheques,* was something my grandfather said to her. If my grandfather loved the color of some of her children more than others. If my father was one of them. If he ever told his children stories. If ever, en escondidas, he met men and women who savored him and made him think his skin was worthy of tasting like salt and leather, a mouthful of buche. If both she and him ever loved the same men in the telenovelas they watched together. If he ever learned to touch himself. If he was ever happy. If he ever felt pretty. If sleeping in a separate bedroom from her was an act of mercy or cruelty. If ever, she finally felt touched by him. If ever he understood that pleasure and liberation in his life did not exist separately from hers. If her fading memory is her body's attempt to forget him and remember peace. If now that she does not recognize him he is afraid to die.

...

These questions which my grandmother will never read or respond to, do not illustrate my desire to finally get to the answer, to the uncovering of any singular originary wound of inherited colonized masculinity, but are rather questions my body asks as I read Ridge's novel and peel the layers of multiple intra-generational silent stories of failed solidarity between competing masculinities interlaced within the retold myth of Joaquín Murrieta and again in Ridge's interplayed life. I say "masculinities" of color and not "men" of color because I am thinking about how colonized bodies both resist and reproduce the violent gendering imposed on them based on their proximity to institutionalized forms of whiteness and racist patriarchy. The unasked questions to my grandmother offer me a strategy for reading the gendered forms of domination I have also been complicit in perpetuating. They are my letting go of the desire to write my father's future from my privileged position of power, are acts of forgiveness, are reckoning, are me looking for another path, are a holding space for other colonized masculinities that dream in feminist solidarity. Reading Ridge's novel opens me up to a knowledge of unknowing the past, one that tells me sometimes to begin healing from a wound, we have to cut it deeper. To cut into the story of Joaquín is to inhabit the space of the dried-out arroyo where Joaquín died and to write in the not visible water the tension between languages that clash in each word I set to write alongside Ridge's. To cut is to ask my body what it knows about how patriarchy moves in language and keeps us from each other. To cut into the dehiscence of the language I speak is not to distinguish a singular alternative language that will liberate me of patriarchy or to speculate one that could have freed Ridge, but to instead imagine it possible to keep opening up our past failures so we can imagine future structures of betrayal committed to failing the bordering language that produced us.

...

What language did we inherit at the margin? Our mouths have failed before. I'm at a conference intended for high school English teachers and community college professors of English hosted by Moreno Valley College. I meet a fellow Chicano. Let's call him Joaquín. He's passionate. The kind of Chicano who believes that his grandfather had to have been an Aztec. The kind of Chicano scholar who believes that the border crossed him. He's ready to liberate la raza at his campus, which is located atop stolen Cahuilla and Luiseño lands that he doubly steals to call Aztlán. He notes the multiple forms of daily racism white teachers enact on Chicanx and Latinx students. I share my anger with him. I am angry. The topic of the conference: "How to engage culturally relevant material." He understands when we talk about our Black and Brown students that we must help them see themselves in the classroom. "We must create a home for them," he says. Later in the day, the conference organizers engage the topic of teaching "culturally relevant material" to include gender and sexuality in our classes. He speaks of a queer Chicano at his campus who comes to his class everyday with makeup and says, "He's asking to be bullied. With all that makeup, he's just asking to get stared at. I don't know how I'm going to talk about gender with him there." All queer people of color collapse into the recesses of his revolution. The Chicano draws his home.

I think to myself, is this why I have failed for so long to call myself Chicano?

Nobody at the table we are sitting at during the conference questions him as he explains his discomfort with queer folks. They are all white. His grammar matches theirs. I cringe at his heteropatriarchal syntax. He draws a neat map for his own liberation and makes intentional choices to perfect his freedom. He thinks he is opening the terrain of the English classroom and working against its institutionalized setting. But as his sentences shift from the present to an impossible future he cannot imagine, *I don't know how I'm going to talk about gender with him there,* he closes the space again and keeps the institution intact by excising queer students from the time-space of his Chicano nation. Whiteness does its job, straightening out his sentences, his body, and his queer student's body. Queer people are his canvas. They make his map of domination possible. But queer folks are also his frontera: his unnecessary comma, and, or, fragment, and, or run-on. For a second I fall into the trap. I want to be included in his sentence. I want his recognition. But his grammar requires that we both be the same subject verbing to the same desires. My desire to be represented, to have the capacity to negotiate my identity and power in his sentence, is a part of the problem. I have to give up my difference in exchange for his validation. I could only belong if I turn away from the colonized and render the boundaries of his heterosexual geography legit. I turn my back to him, refuse him, and as I walk away from him the mirror of myself dissolves. Diffracts into a million possible timelines hidden in the waters beneath the surface of my marginalization.

Joaquín As John Rollin Ridge

And so it begins again with the story of John Rollin Ridge. Unlike most versions of the Murrieta legend, his telling does not actually begin with the bandit's border crossing but with the author's own series of border crossings and encounters with US imperialism that predates the 1848 drawing of the US–Mexican border. In the publisher's preface of *The Life and Adventures of Joaquín Murieta* readers are told John Rollin Ridge's experience would seem to have "well fitted him to portray in living colors the fearful scenes which are described in this book."[1] Ridge is, in other words, not only a writer of the life of Joaquín, but an insightful reader of it and one way to read his story is to read Ridge's life, his body, stitched alongside Joaquín's. The events the preface references quite closely mirror Murrieta's first years in California and serve as a reminder to us readers that the on-going history of Indigenous removal in the US is also a part of Mexican history. The discovery of gold in Georgia, which had prompted the US government to remove the Cherokee, led to the "tragical events" that unfolded in 1835 when John Rollin Ridge's father, also named John Ridge, and his grandfather, Major Ridge, signed the Treaty of New Echota, which ceded lands east

---

1   John Rollin Ridge, *The Life and Adventures of Joaquín Murieta* (New York: Penguin Classics, 1854), 1–2.

of the Mississippi River.[2] The Ridge men believed relocation was inevitable and that through Indian Removal they might secure sovereignty in Indian Territory, if they maintained good relations with the US government. John Ross, a Cherokee Chief who vehemently opposed the Ridges, attempted to dissuade Andrew Jackson from moving forward with the secession. Despite the efforts of Ross and a majority party of Cherokee members, the Cherokee along with Africans they had enslaved were forcibly deported across a new national border, west of the Mississippi river. At the age of twelve, Rollin Ridge, along with his mother and grandmother, witnessed John Ross violently stab John Ridge to death. While Rollin Ridge's Cherokee grandmother stayed in Indian territory, he and his white mother, Sarah Bird Northrup, fled into US territory where he would be educated among white Americans and study law. In 1849, the same year Joaquín crossed the US–Mexican border, Ridge stabbed David Kell, a Ross sympathizer, because he believed Kell was involved with his father's death.

Ridge would then flee to join the Gold Rush in California where the past of his fathers would haunt him. In 1850, shortly after Ridge arrived to California, the state passed the Act for the Government and Protection of Indians which facilitated Indigenous removal from California lands by separating Indigenous communities from their families, languages, and cultures through practices of genocide and enslavement. The law legalized the "indenturing" of Indigenous people and established a system of punishment where "vagrant Indians" who had not yet assimilated could be auctioned off as apprentices and sold to the highest offer from a white bidder. Although California was formally recognized as a state free of slavery after the Compromise of 1850, the alleged "free territory" replicated systems of domination that kept Black and Indigenous people from freedom. In 1852, for example, state legislature passed the California Fugitive

---

2 "Ratified Indian Treaty 199: Cherokee — New Echota, Georgia, December 29, 1835," *National Archives Catalog*, https://catalog.archives.gov/id/183393855.

Slave Law, which legalized the arrest and deportation of runaway enslaved people who arrived with their enslavers before California earned its statehood and status as a "slave free" state.

As Ridge, the son of slaveholders, bore witness to the treatment of Black and California Indigenous populations, Ridge's education and proximity to whiteness as a "mixed-race" Cherokee afforded him the privileges of becoming a writer. He would become the first editor for the Sacramento Bee, and in California he would read newspaper accounts of recently dispossessed Mexicans and write the story of a Mexican man who, after the US had struck gold in California and after the Treaty of Guadalupe Hidalgo was signed by those in power who could also read and write, had also been so terribly wounded by the world of white men.

Joaquín's story seems to have offered Ridge a vehicle by which he could revisit the past and understand the recurring instances of Indigenous and Black removal alongside the onset of failed solidarity among colonized Cherokee men. Although the men who opposed and murdered his father are, in the preface of his text, framed as the "oppressors of his country, who were then in power," the designation of who might have been the oppressed and oppressor, colonizer and colonized, must have left Ridge psychologically rattled after he murdered a fellow Cherokee. We should note, situate, and position the internal community fracture among the Cherokee as emerging from the larger failed solidarity not written out within the pages of his novel: both Major Ridge and John Ridge accumulated their family wealth through slave plantations. There is an incommensurable historical tension between the Ridges as light skinned English-speaking slave owners and the Ridges as colonized subjects whose personhood and sovereignty was constantly denied. Their participation in chattel slavery was deeply tied to the wounded logic of assimilation in the US, where in response to white settlement on their lands the Cherokee adopted slavery, doing as white men did, speaking as white men spoke, because maybe one day white fathers might accept them.

Imani Perry's book, *Vexy Thing,* provides an extensive historical study of the architecture of patriarchy in the US through which we can read the lives the Ridge men led. In her analysis, Perry urges us to understand how systems of slavery positioned non-Black people of color within the architecture of patriarchy based on their varied institutionalized relationships to property ownership. She writes:

> Lower-status possessors of personhood were enlisted to maintain the boundary between personhood and nonpersonhood, both structurally and ideologically, even as their own personhood felt fragile. The boundary formed was always porous, giving those on the margins of personhood even more reason to jealously police it, for fear of slipping under the bar altogether.[3]

The shifting boundary lines of personhood and gender Perry describes were used to map the American landscape and were also woven directly into the grammar of the law. Using similar language that would later shape the Treaty of Guadalupe, the Treaty of New Echota produced a network of gender and racial dominance that granted men like the Ridges with some rights to property as colonized men even as their right to hold it also granted them the right to relinquish it to the US at any moment. Under the ruse of protection, the treaty recognized Cherokee sovereignty in Indian Territory as a domestic space within the nation, still dependent on the authority and guidance of the US. In Article VI of the treaty, for instance, the US promised to "protect the Cherokee nation from domestic strife and foreign enemies and against intestine wars between several tribes." But what the US was really protecting was the right to intervene in Indian territory, should any foreign enemy like Mexico attempt to colonize those Indigenous lands the US might one day desire, should the Cherokee fail to rule themselves, and should

---

3   Imani Perry, *Vexy Thing: On Gender and Liberation* (Durham: Duke University Press, 2018), 52.

non-sovereign Indigenous people already dwelling in Indian Territory threaten the integrity of both nations. In the parallel mapping of "foreign enemies," "domestic strife," and "intestine tribes" as alike threats to the boundaries of Indian Territory, the US conceived of what Jodi Byrd has termed *Indianness*. In her book, *The Transit of Empire*, Byrd describes the process of US settler colonialism as having produced across time the idea of the "Indian" and "Indianness" in order to repeatedly chart territories that could secure the boundaries of white dominance.[4] By incorporating the Cherokee as domestic sovereigns under the patriarchal order of the nation, the Cherokee were racialized in close proximity to "civilized" whiteness and thus distinguished from non-recognized "savage Indians" who, unlike the Ridges, had yet to gain English literacy in boarding schools.

Major Ridge believed that in order to survive US imperialism, his son, Rollin Ridge's father, would have to learn English to engage in political leadership. He was sent to Foreign Mission School, a seminary dedicated to "educating youths of Heathen nations, with a view to their being useful in their respective countries."[5] The education John Ridge received while attending seminary would shape institutionalized boarding schools meant to assimilate Indigenous peoples in the white supremacist project of US imperialism. It is significant to note that in Article VI of the Treaty of New Echota, the same article that promised to "protect" the Cherokee, the US also promised to "provide teachers for the instruction of Indians." In so doing, the educational project of grammatical English was directly linked to the grammar of the law that enforced white patriarchy on colonized Indigenous people like the Ridges. As the lineage of Ridge leaders not only gained English fluency but also married and had children with white women, they gained social mobilities that pulled them toward the margins of personhood where the

---

4   Jodi Byrd, *The Transit of Empire: Indigenous Critiques of Colonialism* (Minneapolis: University of Minnesota Press, 2011).

5   See Jedidiah Morse, "A Report to the Secretary of War of the United States, on Indian Affairs" (1822), Library of Congress, https://www.loc.gov/resource/gdcmassbookdig.reporttosecretaroomors_0/.

enslaved would never be. At the same time, the elite power the Ridges had was less recognized in the eyes of the nation compared to that of some poor and working-class white men who had the right to stay and move into stolen Indigenous lands. The Ridges oscillated within the intermediary space of the margin, on the edge of manhood, racialized and gendered in relation to white male property owning citizens of the US. But on that vulnerable edge of colonized patriarchy, the Ridge men could still dominate Cherokee women, Indigenous communities who were not yet recognized as sovereigns, and the enslaved Black people they owned.

. . .

Readers of Ridge's novel have tended to deploy the text's representation of Joaquín as a literary man, the histories surrounding Ridge's family, and his own coming into English literacy to debate whether or not the author was in truth an assimilationist.[6] The evidence reader's often pull from the novel are the moments where Ridge figures the "half-breed Cherokee" as the only Indigenous people who might be capable of political resistance alongside the Mexicans, meanwhile tribes like the Kitanemuk, Yokuts, Chumash, Miwok, Nisenan, Patwin, and Maidu populations are not only indiscriminately named "Digger" and "Tejon" Indians regardless of tribal differences but also represented as "cowards" without any capacity for political resistance. At one point in the novel for example, when Joaquín and his band are captured and held hostage by the Tejon Indians, Ridge figures

---

6   See John Carlos Rowe, "Highway Robbery: Indian Removal, the Mexican-American War, and American Identity in *The Life and Times of Joaquín Murieta,*" *NOVEL: A Forum on Fiction* 31, no. 2 (1998): 149–73; Jesse Aleman, "Assimilation and the Decapitated Body Politic in *The Life and Adventures of Joaquín Murieta,*" *Arizona Quarterly* 60, no. 1 (2004): 71–98; Mark Rifkin, "For the Wrongs of Our Poor Bleeding Country: Sensation, Class, and Empire in Ridge's *Joaquín Murieta,*" *Arizona Quarterly* 65, no. 2 (2009): 27; and Shelly Streeby, *American Sensations: Class, Empire, and the Production of Popular Culture* (Berkeley: University of California Press, 2002), 265.

Joaquín as unbothered by his capture, because he views the Tejons as a joke. Ridge writes, "Joaquín looked grim for a while, but finally burst out into a loud laugh at his ridiculous position, and ever afterwards endured his captivity with a quiet smile."[7] One way to read Joaquín's attitudes about the Tejons is to read them as Ridge's own attitudes about the Indigenous populations in California. But such an interpretation is complicated if we think about how the Ridge family, who were seen as having betrayed the Cherokee community at large for not actively "resisting" the US in Indian removal, nearly mirror the illustrated passivity of the Tejon Indians in the novel. And while there is certainly evidence one might cull from Ridge's life and journalism to come to self-fulfilling answers that would prove that he was an advocate for the melting pot of America, I am skeptical of reading *The Life and Adventures of Joaquín Murieta* only to arrive at such conclusions. How we approach reading the wound of assimilation in this text can risk landlocking both Ridge's and Murrieta's mouths on one side of the border. Put another way, we must engage in the question of Murrieta's assimilation in the novel carefully so as not to reaffirm or reproduce US borders as natural rather than as violent inventions borne out of the grammar of the law that also often leaves us without another story to tell. What if we refused to read the question of assimilation as a means for finding Ridge a guilty advocate for assimilation? What if we read the novel without deporting Ridge on either side of the Mississippi river or his Murrieta on either side of El Río Grande? One possibility opened by this refusal is an alternative engagement with Ridge as a reader and writer, where we read Ridge's assimilation and woundedness by it not as a limit, or an end point in our understanding of his novel, but as a place of possibility opening with alternative steps we can take if we dance on the margins of his pages, in the places not written but spoken somewhere in an unheard register. Rather than only read Ridge and his Murrieta as exceptional minority subjects who represent "the voice of the voiceless" to white readers, and

---

7   Ridge, *Joaquín Murieta*, 34.

rather than read them as subjects who are able to traverse racial, gender, and class lines in the US because they assimilated and can therefore speak in white grammatical English, we might understand their elusiveness — and our inability to pin either of them down today — by attuning ourselves to the flood of Chicanx and Indigenous reading and writing practices that disrupt the construction of the border. What if, instead of making the English language Ridge uses respect the border, for those of us readers who have survived the violence of the English classroom, we read the myth of Joaquín as told by Ridge in English to ask what structural limitations institutions and the law impose on writing, reading, and the imagination? What if, instead, we also read the novel for the insurgent moments where Ridge and his Murrieta exceed those limitations?

What feels very precious to me as a reader of Ridge's book and life is that we frame both within a deep understanding of the ongoing psychic and emotional ripples of colonization we still feel. A part of feeling that pain necessitates that we linger in, rather than resolve, the difficult contradictions that rift Ridge's life and his writing about Joaquín. Difficult wounds can open timelines. By allowing more possibilities than one be true about Ridge and his book, we allow room for our curiosity and for our exploring the fractures of life and death that lead us nowhere and everywhere. In telling the pieces of myself and my father in my retelling of Ridge's story, I've been attempting to write with, and read with, what I see as Ridge's own defiant genre-bending memoir writing practice, one that engages an Indigenous practice Michelle Raheja has termed "autobiographical disruption." For Raheja, reading early Native American autobiographies that were published in English and in dialogue with competing white literary practices require that we attune ourselves to the "silences and disruptions" Indigenous writers mark in the text. She writes, "What is left unsaid and the kinds of disruptions produced in American Indian autobiographies often reveal more about indigenous resistance, colonial hegemony, and tribal self-life narrative than what is on the page."[8] In this way, with-holding information from the reader is an Indigenous survival strategy whereby the autobiographical subject makes a strategic choice to "hide from view" and to "resist representation" under the white reader's gaze. Although Ridge's novel is not an autobi-ography, his decision to tell the story of Joaquín Murrieta while he also formally instructs us to read his life in the preface that begins and precedes Murrieta's tale, suggests that Ridge's novel contributes to the disruptive writing strategies that characterize Indigenous autobiography even as he also bends the genre by writing about someone who does not necessarily resemble him and by also writing a novel that contributes to the construction of Chicanx identity and myth.

Activated in Ridge's narrative is an Indigenous semi-autobi-ographical Chicanx performance that reveals to us, if not alle-gorizes, the costs of recognition under US law. As a reader I feel the silent palimpsestic Cherokee histories that both undergird and make the book possible as offering a strategy for identify-ing the limits of—and abandoning any desire for—Chicanx identities that rely on patriarchal recognition under any nation. The trap of colonial patriarchy is that it can convince us that we will be free once we receive validation from men, and par-ticularly white men. What Ridge's text seems to do is bring to-gether two historical moments to study how recognition under the law produces failed solidarity between communities of color by positioning people of color in power struggles with one an-other. Ridge's representation of Three-Fingered Jack's violence directed at Chinese miners who do not speak English but who howl and shriek is a horrifying example of how desire for rep-resentation under the Treaty of Guadalupe leaves the Chicano imagination bereft:

---

8   Michelle Raheja, "'I Leave It with the People of the United States to Say': Autobiographical Disruption in the Personal Narratives of Black Hawk and Ely S. Parker," *American Indian Culture and Research Journal* 30, no. 1 (2006): 88.

Three-Fingered Jack, by a nod from Joaquín, stepped up to each one of them and led him out by his long tail of hair, repeating the ceremony until they all stood together in a row before him. He then tied their tails securely together, searched their pockets, while Pedro ransacked their tents, and, drawing his highly-prized home-made knife, commenced amid the howling and shrieks of the unfortunate Asiatics, splitting their skulls and severing their neck-veins. He was in his element, his eyes blazed, he shouted like a madman and leaped from one to the other, hewing and cutting, as if it afforded him the most exquisite satisfaction to revel in human agony.[9]

The antichinismo Three-Fingered Jack specifically aims toward the men's hair establishes a racial hierarchy that cuts across gendering lines. Whether or not Ridge is simply recounting what actually happened in California, his illustration produces a feminized picture of Chinese men and a hypermasculine one of Three-Fingered Jack. The queue hairstyle, the long tail of hair traditionally worn by the Jurchen and Manchu people of China, symbolically registers the men's allegiance to the Qing dynasty and their emperor across the Pacific Ocean. From the novel's vantage point, the men's hair registers the symbolic absent male sovereign who cannot protect them nor legitimize their manhood within the boundaries of the nation. Tying their hair together while *hewing* and *cutting* through their entwined flesh, Joaquín's bloodthirsty right-hand man places the immigrant men outside the nation, floating outside the time and space of post-'48 Mexican and American soil and, therefore, outside of a Chicano political resistance that still depends on US and Mexican territorial boundaries. Jack's racist scope of vision almost prefigures US and Mexican late-nineteenth- and early-twentieth-century practices of Chinese exclusion.[10] Since the immigrant Chinese have no visible male sovereign to recognize

---

9 Ridge, *Joaquín Murieta*, 115.
10 See Jason Oliver Chang, *Chino: Anti-Chinese Racism in Mexico, 1880–1940* (Champaign: University of Illinois Press, 2017).

their rights to property — to declare them as men — the logic of the novel concludes that the Chicanos who have been granted conditional rights through the Treaty of Guadalupe Hidalgo in the US cannot possibly be in solidarity with those who have no recognition in US or Mexican territories at all. That the Chinese are throughout found near the edges of territory, and near deep gorges of water, presumes the immigrant miners as living outside national boundaries, as if they never had made their sojourn across the Pacific Ocean. By severing the Chinese and all other "Asiatics" from Chicano relations, Three-Fingered Jack's cutting of flesh via Joaquín's nod of approval, materially defines the toxic masculine edges of post-'48 Chicano identity; and as the Chinese collapse into a deterritorialized feminine space the Chicano draws his home. In attempting to create a geography of Chicano belonging within the American landscape, the Chicano revolt represented by Ridge brutally replicates the grammar of exclusion repeated in The Treaty of New Echota and again in The Treaty of Guadalupe Hidalgo. By representationally mapping the Chinese as non-sovereigns who are not legally recognized in the US, Ridge's text illustrates how the Chicanos, in this case, gain partial recognition as citizens of the US through settler-colonial practices of patriarchal dominance that also transform and racialize Chinese skulls into symbolic "Indian heads."

...

Three-Fingered Jack's hand, the method of violence he wages against Chinese heads, carries with it multiple colluding histories of US and Mexican violences directed against Indigenous heads before the annexation of Mexican lands and before the congealing of the US border. After the US forcibly deported the Cherokee, Creek, Choctaw, Chickasaw, and Seminole nations into Indian Territory, Apache and Comanche tribes dwelling there on the margins of Mexican territories felt the encroachment of European colonial settlers and displaced eastern Indigenous tribes that left them with very little resources. As consequence, the Apache and Comanche pushed their boundaries further south and raided the northern Mexican states of Sonora, Chihuahua, and Coahuilla for resources. Vulnerable to Apache raiding and US imperialism, Mexico sought to define its borders through a vision of mestizaje that only embraced Indigenous people abstractly. Indigenous cultural differences were erased within a Mexican identity defined by the mixed bloodline of Spanish and Indian mestizaje that praised the eventual blanqueamiento of the mestize race. By inventing mestize identity, Mexico could refuse territorial accommodations for Indigenous tribes like the Apache and Comanche who resisted identifying as mestizes. This exacerbated the Apache wars against northern Mexico and between 1845–1885 northern Mexican states engaged in a transnational alliance with the US by installing bounty programs along the border for the scalping and beheading of Apache and Comanche tribes who were deemed unassimilable in the white US and in mestize Mexico. The northern Mexican state from where Joaquín Murrieta migrated, Sonora, for example, attracted people from both sides of the border, rewarding mestizes, afromestizes, Cherokee and Seminole tribes from Indian Territory, and enslaved African Americans, who were promised the freedoms of mestize Mexican identity in exchange for Apache heads. Meanwhile, the US viewed the Apache wars on the northern frontier as an opportunity to expand its borders into Mexico. By inciting the US–Mexican war, the US had an advantage over a northern Mexico depleted of financial resources in the fight against the Apache. After the war, the US promised relief to northern Mexico by continuing to wage war against Indians that threatened both nations along the border.[11] Through shared practices of Indian beheadings, the treaty attempted peace between Mexico and the US.

But the war between both nations was forever. The newly annexed Mexicans still living in the US fell victim to the historical residues of both Mexican and US histories of anti-Indigenous violence. If anyone looked "Mexican" they could be stopped

11   María Josefina Saldaña-Portillo, *Indian Given: Racial Geographies across Mexico and the United States* (Durham: Duke University Press, 2016).

at any moment on the street by any white man who wanted them beaten, shot, or lynched. At hang parties, white children held their gazes up above their parents faces where our bodies dangled under trees, our heads constellations they could never reach.

...

Tommy Orange's debut 2019 novel *There There* begins by connecting Indigenous beheadings that took place in California to the story of Joaquín Murrieta's beheading as told by John Rollin Ridge. He writes:

> The first novel by a Native person, the first novel written in California, was written in 1854, by a Cherokee guy named John Rollin Ridge. *The Life and Adventures of Joaquín Murieta* was based on a supposed real-life Mexican bandit from California by the same name, who was killed by a group of Texas rangers in 1853. To prove they'd killed Murieta and collect the $5,000 reward put on his head — they cut it off. Kept it in a jar of whiskey. They also took the hand of his fellow bandit Three-Fingered Jack. The rangers took Murieta's head and Jack's hand on tour throughout California, charged a dollar for the show.

> The Indian head in the jar, the Indian head on a spike were like flags flown, to be seen, cast broadly.[12]

By opening a novel that details contemporary Indigenous life in Oakland, California with Ridge's writing and the myth of Joaquín, Orange's text calls for remembering the lynching of Mexicans in California as inextricably linked to the transnational histories of Indigenous genocide that still shape the present. Such a revision to the dominant myth puts us Chicanes in check by refiguring Joaquín's beheading, as it is traditionally

---

12 Tommy Orange, *There There* (New York: Knopf, 2018), 5.

used to tell the story of wrongs done to Chicanes in the US, by instead having us reckon Joaquín's death at the hands of Anglos alongside unaccounted for Indigenous deaths at the hands of Mexicans and Chicanes. To remember Joaquín's life and death, for Orange, is to remember an Indigenous landscape of survival in California concealed by historical amnesia. He writes:

> We are the memories we don't remember, which live in us, which we feel, which make us sing and dance and pray the way we do, feelings from memories that flare and bloom un-expectedly in our lives like blood through a blanket from a wound made by a bullet fired by a man shooting us in the back for our hair, for our heads, for bounty, or just to get rid of us.[13]

...

To remember the Indigenous relations that have been cut off from Joaquín, we have to go back to the water that cuts through the patriarchal landscape the Chicanos draw in Ridge's novel. After a group of Americans hunt down a group of Tejon Indians who have allegedly stolen their horses at the start of the narrative, the Americans "hem them between a perpendicular wall of bluffs and a deep river, so that there was no escape for them but to swim the stream, which swept by in a mad and foaming torrent."[14] The Americans shoot and as the Indians jump into the river nearly all of them are killed and their blood dyes the river red. It is only after Tejon flesh and blood intermingle with the river that Joaquín and his Mexican band make their settlement and establish their headquarters in Arroyo Cantoova, a mestize landscape that occasionally floods with water and, sometimes, Indigenous blood. Although we are told one of Joaquín's Mexican men, who had been leading the Tejons, dies with them at the river, the sequence of events in the novel seem to indicate

---

13 Ibid., 10.
14 Ridge, *Joaquín Murieta*, 23–24.

that native death at water will secure Chicano representation in California territory. Time and again throughout Ridge's book, it is near the edges of territory, near rivers and streams and arroyos, where Joaquín and his band abandon the communities who would otherwise assist them in their revolt. Because unlike the Chicanos, the other communities of color represented in the novel have not been promised citizenship and political recognition under the law, they are dismembered, forgotten: the Tejons are left to die in rivers, the Chicanas are abandoned near Arroyo Cantua, and the Chinese are slaughtered near deep gorges of water.

But if Ridge's novel documents the failed solidarity and violence between communities of color produced under the grammar of the law, it is near water that the map of US territory cannot draw a limit and where undercurrents for insurgent solidarity and social upheaval still live. Now while the revolt Ridge documents fails particularly because the Chicanos choose to seek recognition under the law rather than to draw bridges across racial, ethnic, and gendered differences, Ridge's novel nonetheless scores the page with the possibility that solidarity might have happened if we listen to the timelines refracted in water. It's near water where we might come to realize that recognition under patriarchal national borders is not the aim or end point. It's while Joaquín and his bandits are near water that Ridge highlights the potentialities of water: its capacity to reshape the land and to defy any boundary line. Its ability to disguise both Ridge and Murrieta from the white colonial gaze. One of the most striking and in-depth descriptions Ridge provides of the California geography showcases how the land that has quite literally been cut and molded by water provides the Chicanes with a place where they might dwell without the threat of white men intent on deporting them. He writes about Chaparral Hill at length by detailing the following:

> It lies to the southwest of San Andreas about four miles, and is nothing more than an elevated pass between two steep ridges, which are crowned with precipitous rocks whose in-

terstices would effectual conceal a man from observation. Thickets of chaparral cover various spots on the tops of the ridges, with open spaces between, and, in many places, the live-oak trees, with low branches and crooked, knotty trunks, form a kind of natural fortification, almost as perfect as if they had been arranged expressly for the purpose. The pass itself is but a lowering of a long curving wall, (a natural wall) which connects the two ridges together, and, between these ridges, a long hollow leads up and terminates at the pass. By the foot of the hollow runs a clear little stream margined with green grass, called Willow Creek, because it is fringed so beautiful with the lithe and graceful trees of that name. Behind the curving wall described, a steep descent goes down to the valley below, and is covered with immense greasewood thickets, taller than a man's head, through which a party pursued could make a most safe retreat and through which it would be dangerous to follow them. One ridge terminates at the connecting wall, but the other stretches on a mile or two beyond it, marked by bridle trail which suddenly plunges into a succession of deep ravines and gulches lined with greasewood and low timber — lonely, and sombre-looking places! From this pass, or any place adjacent, a view of the country is commanded many miles in extent.[15]

One cannot help but notice Ridge activate his name in the entire description of the hill: the steep ridges that lie at the intersection of mountains, the ridges that open up space for trees to grow, the ridges that create long hollow passes, terminate walls, open other paths. To make a ridge requires that the land be broken by the rush and flood of rain from above or by the conflicting undercurrents that move below, out of sight and without mercy. When the plates beneath the ground flow and slip, the ridges of mountain ranges and unending hills take shape. Millions of years ago, the San Andreas Mountains rose above the ground as the plates beneath the sea and sand slipped over one another

---

15 Ridge, *Joaquín Murieta,* 99–100.

forming what we now call the San Andreas fault. Theorists of plate tectonics believe that one day the plates will move and that all of California will make its return beneath sea level, as it had been before a million and more years ago. Ridge gives his name and body over to the torrent of shifting fault lines, where his name might be deranged by the edges of time and water. And it's our mouths, the tongues of his readers, who are made to utter his name as it has been shaped by an endless ribbon that sloughs, marks, and tears. Natalie Díaz writes, "I am fluent in water. Water is fluent in my body — it spoke my body into existence."[16] Reclaiming water as indigenous to her Mojave language, land, and body, Díaz's fluid tongue offers a method for reading the language Ridge uses to write his name in the passage above. Speaking in water, he marks the page with saturated meanings not locked down by the territorial colonial boundaries that wounded his fathers. Somewhere in that spillage is his refusal to be recognized by any father.

Somewhere in that nowhere time puddles, swells above the banks of linear time so Ridge can meet and touch Murrieta. Anywhere water is held on Earth is a healing place that was once an open wound. Gulches and ravines know this. They are always healing, waiting to be filled and emptied again, marked by the slippery footsteps that come and go. Only sometimes, do our bodies know the power of this wayward waiting dance. Ridge must have known this because his Joaquín knows it and, sometimes, trusts the knowledge of water. He and his band only survive for so long because the white men cannot catch them in lands they have not mapped. As they remain and linger close to the water, they cannot be recognized. At one point, Ridge takes our eyes high above in bird's-eye view so that we can see how Joaquín and his band remain hidden because the bottom of the creeks and rivers have been so deeply lacerated by time. When Joaquín and his men attempt to steal a sailing ship running through Calaveras County headed toward San Francisco,

---

16 Natalie Díaz, "Exhibits from the American Water Museum," in *Postcolonial Love Poem* (Minneapolis: Graywolf Press, 2020), 69.

Ridge writes, "He at last saw the white-sheeted schooner steal-
ing along in the crooks and turns of just the crookedest stream
in the whole world, so narrow and so completely hid in its wind-
ings by the tall flags which overspread the plains for many miles
to the right and left, the white sail looked like a ghost gliding
along the waving grass."[17] Both running water and the body of
the boat are veiled from those looking high above along the
mountain ranges and down below from those on the flatlands.
It's no surprise then that Ridge's Joaquín spends most of his time
near the water that bends the land by refusing to stay in one
place for too long. It's strategic. To mimic the transgression of
water is to refuse being straightened out and legibly seen, like
a letter on a page. Smeared ink in the flood stretch of aqueous
movement, somewhere between the word "crooked" turned into
the superlative "crookedest," is an endless encounter with fragments of time.

...

Where I grew up, I was cut by
dirt light washes circling
the half-dried rocks along the Sacramento, American, and Cosumnes rivers,

where the sweat below the canopy
where the slow panting oaks

still whisper:
fuck the border.
Where thornwater brushed my lips
I opened
Drank in hills   I could not stop
I could not stop
I cannot stop
Pulling
fingertips

---

17   Ridge, *Joaquín Murieta*, 61.

dripping from our bloodied mouths

below the moonlight flooding
our stage light from above

My throat opens
swells into your gourd
releases you
into my palm spread wide
drowning enough to catch as many digging seconds.

the river's black cloak belts a wailing gurgle:
nunca, parale, forever

where the salmon swimming in its watershed of time lived in
the word, before, dying after they left the ocean to migrate back
home to rivers, spawning where they were spawned

before and after
enduring.

Where I grew up, the Miwok dwelling along the banks of the
Cosumnes River believed, and still do, that before earth there
was only water.

Water is time dancing
the rest,
rests,
escapes.

...

Some days, when I'm feeling hopeless, I'm afraid to admit that
I feel you even when you are not there. Some days, I'm afraid
to ask whether or not I will ever meet you in this timeline. And
maybe that's why I'm writing to you about this book I read about
wounded men wounding wounded men in the first place: be-

cause I feel like I've already lost you this time. Because for years all I wanted was for you to see me. Because I hadn't learned that my desire to be seen by you is what kept us from seeing each other. I should say keeps. Por dios.

You used to pray for me in the morning. In my doorway before you left for work. Enveloped by darkness, and not yet pulled out of my dreams, I would peer one eye open, feel your presence, the silhouette of you caused by the hallway light and hear you whisper a "Padre Nuestro." Your words, entering mis sueños, Padre Nuestro, how lost I am looking for you in the light. If shadows could claim the body I know I'd love you better.

I think about the time you should have seen me standing in that gorgeous striped black and blue tutu among fallen crayons, apple juice boxes with bent straws, papers with hand drawn images of stick figure families, green dinosaurs, purple fairies, rainbows, and birds only the young could see. As the remaining group of children scrambled for the remaining costumes I did not select from the cardboard box, the spandex I held between my fingers felt like skin I could carefully slip into. One leg first, then the other, up over my belly button and over my shoulders. Picture me free, unaware, like the other children giggling not out of fear but delight drawn from my choice. Picture the crayon I dropped to paint my body powerful. Picture me as I choose to remember me now before I was straightened out, swimming in blue and black streams, plunged into depths dancing all around me as I twirl with the desire all children have to continue becoming themselves at every endless second, every endless hour, without an adult who will stop time for boys dancing in tutus.

Imagine me. Imagine me dancing and tiptoeing and bringing my arms out wide, claiming every inch in the classroom. There must have been a mirror from where I can remember what I looked like because I can see it so clearly now: the aquamarine blur of myself, and behind my reflection, the horrified expression of my kindergarten teacher looking from his thin-rimmed glasses. How far back in time do I have to rewind so you can meet me here, at this moment, before my teacher recognizes what he does not want to see, and from where you can also twirl beside me. How far do I have to extend my reach for us to touch each other in relentless motion without eyes that will keep us from meeting.

…

Sometimes when I remember my mother's language I can make the world move slow enough and on rare occasions I can listen to the objects from the memory of my childhood visits in Atecucario that bring me close to touching you. The water I drank from the cantaro in my grandmother nena's kitchen, which left the thick taste of clay on my tongue; the way nenita arranged plantitas near the windows so that they would get enough sunlight; the pilled tangled threads on the worn out couch in the living room, the texture of an overwashed sweater; the disconnected bedrooms and bathrooms that made the house feel like it was not a house; the warm summer rain that left me drenched as I moved from the living room to the outdoor kitchen and stove still warmed by firewood; the smell of pumice and soap in the air of the washroom; the roosters crowing in the early morning, the dogs howling deep into the night; the midnight chatter of lovers lingering by the sidewalk, an endless porch connecting all the colorful houses paled by darkness.

I can feel you now. You are eight years old and needy. By around this time, your brothers have started to call you "la gallina" because you are too chicken to go to the outdoor bathroom alone at night. Tired of their relentless teasing, you retreat into yourself, somewhere small within where you can still feel safe in your body. While your brothers roll in the dirt and pigshit and tear through the clothes your mother has just patched up, you wander near the outdoor kitchen and washroom, at the edge of the world of women, waiting for your father to come home from la milpa and your mother to return from selling tamales en la plaza.

The sopping and scouring sounds draw you into the washroom where you find mi tía Leti. Before you notice her, you wince at the sight of your sister's red palms. Because you are still a boy, you offer to help and, together, join the music she makes. "Mira niño, asina se asé," I can hear my tía Leti instructing you. Asina, that rhythmic word I only know out of my tíos y tías from Michoacán. Asina, a word combined out of the phrase, así nada más, or así no más, defying every grammar rule and translating imperfectly to, *like this,* or *like this no more no less, just like this,* or *just like that.* Asina, the word, a blend of phrases, instructs you to look closely, to pay attention to the way Leti dunks the t-shirt into soapy water, wrings it, slaps it down against the ribbed slab of stone, scrubs both sides with enough force to rinse and enough care not to tear. Each step of the process coming together like water. "Asina, niño," she says once more and this time you follow her lead.

Epilogue
Reading with My Students

I came to reflect the ideas presented in this book as I taught John Rollin Ridge's canonical nineteenth-century American novel, *The Life and Adventures of Joaquín Murieta,* in the fall of 2019 during my first year as a tenure-track English Professor at Cosumnes River College. As I read the novel along with my students, I realized that the historical failed solidarity between communities of color that we were examining in the text was also unfolding right in front of me in my very own English department. I became heightened to the ways in which academic writing has wounded and harmed our lives as professors and students in really profound ways and in my writing I had to confront how wounded I was. In other words, I was forced to look at how much I wanted to write for my students but how much I had been trained to do the opposite of that.

When I was hired in fall 2018 at CRC, I had expectations for what solidarity and coalition might look like among students and faculty of color. After having built a tight-knit community at UC Riverside with rebellious graduate students in the English department I belonged to, I expected something similar to manifest at my new job. I learned early on from my first department meetings, however, that the structure of the university had never made solidarity possible for me in graduate school. My friends and I did that. The structure of every university, I would learn, depended on faculty of color betraying one another in their commitment to academic English literacy and grammar.

Perhaps like many classroom activists who land their first tenure-track job, however, I hoped as I walked into my first department meeting that I would still bind to my colleagues of color and that, together, we would incite revolt against the white supremacist structures of the English classroom. I was excited to bring all the queer of color theory I had read in graduate school into this place. To put theory into practice would surely happen here at a predominantly Black and Latinx serving institution that constantly champions what I now recognize as a coercive phrase and motto, "Diversity Is Our Strength." Diversity and inclusion into an already broken system of course guaranteed that I would be disappointed to meet colleagues of color who had been so harmed by the university and their own experiences in graduate school that they replicated that harm. I was initially horrified by some of the first attitudes I heard about student writing both within and outside of the English department. I met faculty who prided themselves on the difficulty of their students getting an A in their courses. "Did they survive?" a colleague of mine once asked sinisterly after I told them that a family member of mine had taken their writing course years ago. I met folks who spoke of English language learners as if they would never pass college English. I was challenged by colleagues who believed that students with learning disabilities would be met with failure instead of asking themselves about how we, as faculty, have yet to be trained in teaching students with disabilities or how these disabilities might have emerged from the trauma our students experienced in their K-12 education and would continue to experience in our own ignorance. I was, furthermore, confronted by faculty that believed their students were in perpetual despair, always suffering, always impaired, always illiterate, always Black and Brown, waiting for a white professor, or a professor of color with just the right amount white respectability, class, and impeccable grammar, who might save them. And I couldn't help but think, it sounds like we the faculty are in need of some saving.

The attitudes I encountered at CRC were not new, however. I had heard them in my five years of teaching when I worked at UC Riverside as a graduate student and in my two years working as an adjunct for Moreno Valley Community College. Nonetheless, I could not help but feel a certain antagonism towards the colleagues of color I felt were perpetuating harm at my college. This was before I fully acknowledged and saw how much pain my colleagues were in and before I checked how my presence at CRC, as a professor who teaches queer of color feminist thought in English composition and literature classrooms, might be what generational privilege looks like. It is because of the women of color in my department, and the fights they fought before I joined the department that I even had a chance to enter this space. But I could not have anticipated, nor have been fully aware, how harmed the women in my department were. As Lisa, a colleague and dear friend of mine, recently told me about her experience as one of the first women of color in the English department, "I was just trying to survive those years." As I spoke out against the tyrannies of the university and attempted to create a collaborative queer feminist anti-racist healing space, I had to note that the women of color in my department might have also visioned something similar at some point along their academic careers but could never voice that vision without the threat of losing their jobs, even after having gained tenure.

When I have tried to express these feelings of isolation and failed solidarity between faculty of color to white faculty members throughout my years of teaching, often they believe my logic is flawed because I am basing an assumed solidarity with colleagues through skin color. While I can see where my colleagues are headed with their point (that I shouldn't assume white people do not support me), I can tell that they do not understand that I am not talking about what they might call reverse racism, but a shared pain between faculty of color who have been harmed by the institution and the structures of white supremacy that shape every space we enter. I am talking about how faculty of color might commit to the disruption of academic structures for our collective healing. In white faculty responses I keep hearing, *look, I support you more than them.* I hear, *I'm better.* I hear, *don't look over there, look at me.* I turn away from them, looking for the quiet.

What they fail to closely examine is that I am making a point about what it might mean for all of us to betray our situational proximity to whiteness in the university and to commit to a reevaluation of that relational position in the English classroom. I need them to listen. I needed them to learn how to read closely. To do this, they have to address their complicities with institutionalized racism and their own proximity to whiteness as professors who do not experience the same trauma the women, people of color, and queer people of color in our departments have. They have to, in other words, see that their solidarity with me is not possible until they too betray their whiteness and bear witness to the ways in which they have been spared from the instruction that has wounded the faculty of color in our departments who continue to survive the legacies of colonialism. They need to see how their historical position in our college operates as folks of color are pitted against each other in a commitment to a literacy that has made them accomplices to white supremacy.

I should contextualize my initial disappointment in the failed solidarity I witnessed at CRC by saying that I entered my institution at an incredibly fraught moment. But what I really want to say is that it was actually an incredibly fraught moment for the pedagogy of colonial white grammar. In 2018, California passed AB705, a law that required that community colleges allow open access to transfer level English and Math courses by getting rid of remedial and pre-requisite courses that disproportionately impact Black and Latinx students from graduating on time. Additionally, the law pushes community colleges to ensure that students will finish their English and Math GE courses within their first year of attending. These changes led to a slew of other challenges for some faculty across California community colleges who are concerned with the wave of students entering spaces that were previously unavailable to them (namely, students with various language abilities coming from poor and working-class Black, Indigenous, Asian American, and Latinx populations).

When I came to my institution, I was quite happy about the law since one of my most traumatizing experiences I had before coming to CRC was working as a "remedial English" instructor for UC Riverside's University Writing Program. I remember thinking as I entered my classroom, after having taught the "college-ready"-level writing courses students would take after, and after having graded my "remedial" students' first essays, that this is what modern-day segregation looked like. All of my students were capable of being placed in their first-year college composition course. None of them needed to be there; the institution needed them to be there. The university ensured these students would take the same course for two years, quarter after quarter, before they would finally pass, if they did at all.

I was bored the entire time I taught this course. So were the students. Every essay was formulaic. Creativity was stifled, critiqued, killed. I tried my best to sneak in examples of revolutionary queer of color feminist writing by Audre Lorde, Gloria Anzaldúa, and Cherríe Moraga, though I warned them that they could not write like the writers I taught in their final exam because they would be graded by an anonymous racist UWP committee. To train them for their final exam, I taught students in American Standard English (ASE). After ten weeks with me, students had to take a timed written exam that would be graded not by their instructors but by instructors they had never met and who had been taught under the monolith of ASE. I was among the instructors who would grade a stack of papers that were not from my own students. As I sat at the grade norming session the morning before we would grade, I saw beneath the mask of "unbiased grading," the fact that this was really just "racist grading." Among the stacks of student examples, we all read one essay by a Mexican student that tied the dull prompt about architecture to their own cultural experiences with the architecture of the pyramids in México. The student described how rituals would be performed at these sites to defend the significance of the architecture. The leader of our grade norming session scoffed. He used the word "savage" to describe the student's experience. He gave it a D because the student "diverged" from the prompt. The student would have to re-enroll in English 4 again the following semester. I wanted to run.

I passed nearly everyone in my stack of anonymous students. Because my own students were going to be graded under these terms, I told them on the first day of class to make sure to complete all of their assignments and to come to class every day because it would help balance out their final grade based on their participation grade. The final grade was not determined by myself but a formula that blended the final essay with the final grade they earned in my course. Nearly all of my students had perfect participation scores and many of them also had A's. By the time all of my students took their exams, however, all of those A's were turned to C's based on the UWP Standardized English Rubrics that were used to grade their final exams.

Before my grades were turned in, I was called into the UWP office to meet with the director of the University Writing Program. He had looked into my gradebook online and had determined that my participation scores were much too high. There were "too many A's" in my class. I told him that my students had earned these grades and that I also didn't understand the concept of there ever being a shortage of A's students could earn in one class. He suggested that I lower them. I told him I would take a look again at my gradebook to see if some of them needed to change. I said this so he would leave me alone, but I had no intention of doing so. Before the meeting ended, he continued to make small talk with me about my dissertation. I told him that I was writing about Herman Melville. As I said this to him, I could not help but revisit all those years of my schooling when English teachers praised me for having read a white American author and I feared that I might now, years later, be perceived as their American Dream: the son of Mexican immigrants not only writing about Melville but colonizing other Black and Brown students. Before leaving his office, I turned around and, perhaps speaking to the sum of my English teachers, specified that I was writing about queer Latinx worlds in Melville's work. I don't think it made a difference, but I wanted control over how I was remembered.

When I got home, I submitted my grades later that week as they already were. And when I returned the following semester I found a letter in my mailbox from the UWP notifying me that I had breached my contract and failed my obligations as an instructor. The letter served as a warning. That was the last class I taught for the UWP. After that I left the UWP and thankfully taught for the English Literature department at UCR. Shortly after that, I moved back to Sacramento to teach at CRC. The year after I left, the UWP was confronted by students of color who filed a grievance on its racist practices and honestly, by the time that case was opened, I was thankful I had left Riverside and that I was at an institution that had just gotten rid of their remedial English equivalent course because of AB705.

The miracle of AB705 is that I am teaching material that I have longed to teach to my students of color for a really long time, especially reading material that I know has previously been withheld from them. The failure of AB705 is that the law, of course, cannot completely change how English professors approach students in the classroom based on the way they have been trained, for generations, to become white colonizers. A central concern for my department, for example, has been the question about the continued centralization of American and British Literature as a graduation requirement for the English major and the simultaneous gatekeeping of these courses. Before the spring of 2021, the only English courses in my department that continued to have prerequisites were American and British Literature. This means students had to take their first-year writing class before they could read American and British Literature, but they were well off to take Race and Ethnicity in Contemporary American Literature, Native American Literature, Latinx Literature, LGBTQ+ Literature, Women in Literature, and African American Literature courses without a single prerequisite barrier. I bumped up against necessary questions as my department began discussing whether or not to keep prerequisites for American and British Literatures: What does it mean to claim students are not "literate enough" before they are allowed to take a course? What does it mean that the distinction between which courses require prerequisites and which do not are clearly drawn across racial, gendered, classed, and sexual lines? Additionally, who are we keeping out of our American and British Literature courses? Of course the answer was in my own Latinx Literature classroom in the fall of 2019 where my students of color were reading Ridge's *Joaquín Murieta*. And it was my students, as they examined the structure of whiteness and patriarchy in the novel, that were helping me read and narrate what was going on with my colleagues. They were giving language to the structures they were both inhabiting but were also being kept from recognizing and naming.

My decision to teach Ridge's *Joaquín Murieta* not in an American Literature course but in a Latinx Literature course that had not been offered until I taught it in 2019 was a political choice. When I created the course, I made sure there were no prerequisites, meaning any student could enroll in this course no matter their level of literacy or ability to write in American Standard English or training to cite things in MLA format. *Joaquín Murieta,* which is more likely to be taught in an American Literature course than a Latinx Literature course, is a text that students would otherwise not get the chance read because they are not yet "literate enough." Despite my attempted revolt, I too fell prey to this question of who was "literate enough" when one of my students came into my course knowing very little to no English. She dropped the course about halfway through the semester. Because this was an "English Literature" course and because it was my first year on the tenure track, I was afraid to teach this course in spanglish and to create the conditions for this student to feel comfortable enough to interpret the text, even if her interpretations were in Spanish. At the end of the course, my students asked what happened to this student and when I told them that I thought she dropped because she didn't know much

English, they stated that they wished they could have helped her translate and tutor her. I realize now that I, caring more about my survival within the institution, and my own tenure, failed my student in this moment and the collective magic my other students would have created with her. Was this not the dream course I always hoped for as an ESL student growing up? As I look back on this failed moment, I see the work I still have to do, to rid myself of the shame I feel when speaking my languages within the classroom setting and with inviting my students to this place inside me that the institution had tried to kill in me.

One of my students in my Latinx Literature course told me that semester that he was surprised to hear how fluent I was in Spanish when I helped his mother at the Reading and Writing Center on campus. This was the first time he had heard me speak full sentences in Spanish. Even in an English class I was afraid to open up this course for plurilingual practice. But what Carlos, Trinity, Angelisa, Shannon, Guillermo, Leticia, Omar, Gabriela, Alejandro, Joey, Cynthia, and Daniel helped me see that semester as we read *Joaquín* in the same classroom where I took my very first college level English composition class in room T116 nine years before was that the institution that gave birth to me, that made me, was still doing its work to try and keep me from them. Every week we sat and tried our best to destroy the literary scholar that I was supposed to reproduce in them and that had been produced in me. Together, we began reading.

To my students, for teaching me how to write this book, I am forever in your debt.

Bibliography

Alemán, Jesse. "Assimilation and the Decapitated Body Politic
    in *The Life and Adventures of Joaquín Murieta*." *Arizona
    Quarterly: A Journal of American Literature, Culture, and
    Theory* 60, no. 1 (2004): 71–98. DOI: 10.1353/arq.2004.0014.
Anzalduá, Gloria. *Borderlands: The New Mestiza = La Frontera.*
    San Francisco: Aunt Lute Books, 1987.
Bambara, Toni Cade. "Foreword to the First Edition, 1981." In
    Gloria Anzaldúa and Cherríe Moraga, *This Bridge Called My
    Back*, xxix. Fourth edition. New York: SUNY Press, 2015.
Brady, Mary Pat. *Extinct Lands, Temporal Geographies:
    Chicana Literature and the Urgency of Space.* Durham: Duke
    University Press, 2002.
Byrd, Jodi A. *The Transit of Empire: Indigenous Critiques of
    Colonialism.* Minneapolis: University of Minnesota Press,
    2011.
Chang, Jason Oliver. *Chino: Anti-Chinese Racism in Mexico,
    1880–1940.* Champaign: University of Illinois Press, 2017.
Diaz, Natalie. *Postcolonial Love Poem: Poems.* Minneapolis:
    Graywolf Press, 2020.
Flores, Nelson, and Jonathan Rosa. "Undoing Appropriateness:
    Raciolinguistic Ideologies and Language Diversity in
    Education." *Harvard Educational Review* 85, no. 2 (2015):
    149–71. DOI: 10.17763/0017-8055.85.2.149.

Gonzales-Day, Ken. *Lynching in the West, 1850–1935*. Durham: Duke University Press, 2006.

Gurba, Myriam. *Mean*. Minneapolis: Coffee House Press, 2017.

Harney, Stefano, and Fred Moten. *The Undercommons: Fugitive Planning and Black Study*. London: Minor Compositions, 2013.

Heizer, Robert F., and Alan J. Almquist. *The Other Californians: Prejudice and Discrimination under Spain, Mexico, and the United States to 1920*. Berkeley: University of California Press, 2000.

hooks, bell. *The Will to Change: Men, Masculinity, and Love*. New York: Washington Square Press, 2004.

Leal, Luis. "El Corrido de Joaquín Murrieta: Origen y Difusión." *Mexican Studies/Estudios Mexicanos* 11, no. 1 (1995): 1–23. DOI: 10.1525/msem.1995.11.1.03a00010.

Lorde, Audre. *Zami: A New Spelling of My Name*. New York: Crossing Press, 1982.

Moraga, Cherríe. *Loving in the War Years: Lo Que Nunca Pasó Por Sus Labios*. Boston: South End Press, 2000.

Moraga, Cherríe, and Gloria Anzaldúa, eds. *This Bridge Called My Back: Writings by Radical Women of Color*. Fourth edition. New York: SUNY Press, 2015.

Morse, Jedidiah. "A Report to the Secretary of War of the United States, on Indian Affairs" (1822). *Library of Congress*. https://www.loc.gov/resource/gdcmassbookdig.reporttosecretaroomors_o/.

Muñoz, José Esteban. *Cruising Utopia: The Then and There of Queer Futurity*. New York: New York University Press, 2009.

Orange, Tommy. *There There*. New York: Alfred A. Knopf, 2018.

Perry, Imani. *Vexy Thing: On Gender and Liberation*. Durham: Duke University Press, 2018.

Pfaelzer, Jean. *Driven Out: The Forgotten War against Chinese Americans*. Berkeley: University of California Press, 2008.

Raheja, Michelle H. "'I Leave It with the People of the United States to Say': Autobiographical Disruption in the Personal

Narratives of Black Hawk and Ely S. Parker." *American Indian Culture and Research Journal* 30, no. 1 (October 2007): 87–108. DOI: 10.17953/aicr.30.1.d44268566777k322.

"Ratified Indian Treaty 199: Cherokee — New Echota, Georgia, December 29, 1835." *National Archives Catalog.* https://catalog.archives.gov/id/183393855.

Ridge, John Rollin, et al. *The Life and Adventures of Joaquín Murieta: The Celebrated California Bandit.* London: Penguin Books, 2018.

Rifkin, Mark. "'For the Wrongs of Our Poor Bleeding Country': Sensation, Class, and Empire in Ridge's *Joaquín Murieta*." *Arizona Quarterly: A Journal of American Literature, Culture, and Theory* 65, no. 2 (June 2009): 27–56. DOI: 10.1353/arq.0.0037.

Rodriguez, Richard. *Days of Obligation: An Argument with My Mexican Father.* London: Penguin Books, 1993.

Rodríguez, Richard T. *Next of Kin: The Family in Chicano/a Cultural Politics.* Durham: Duke University Press, 2009.

Rosa, Jonathan. *Looking Like a Language, Sounding Like a Race: Raciolinguistic Ideologies and the Learning of Latinidad.* Oxford: Oxford University Press, 2019.

Rowe, John Carlos. "Highway Robbery: 'Indian Removal,' the Mexican–American War, and American Identity in 'The Life and Adventures of Joaquín Murieta.'" *NOVEL: A Forum on Fiction* 31, no. 2 (1998): 149–73. DOI: 10.2307/1346196.

Saldaña-Portillo, María Josefina. *Indian Given: Racial Geographies across Mexico and the United States.* Durham: Duke University Press, 2016.

Smith, Stacey L. "Remaking Slavery in a Free State: Masters and Slaves in Gold Rush California." *Pacific Historical Review* 80, no. 1 (2011): 28–63. DOI: 10.1525/phr.2011.80.1.28.

Spillers, Hortense J. "Mama's Baby, Papa's Maybe: An American Grammar Book." *Diacritics* 17, no. 2 (1987): 64–81. DOI: 10.2307/464747.

Streeby, Shelley. *American Sensations: Class, Empire, and the Production of Popular Culture.* Berkeley: University of California Press, 2002.

"Treaty of Guadalupe Hidalgo (1848)." *National Archives.* https://www.archives.gov/milestone-documents/treaty-of-guadalupe-hidalgo.

Wynter, Sylvia. "1492: A New World View." In *Race, Discourse, and the Origin of the Americas: A New World View,* edited by Vera Lawrence Hyatt and Rex Nettleford, 5–57. Washington, DC: Smithsonian Institution Press, 1995.

Printed in the USA
CPSIA information can be obtained
at www.ICGtesting.com
LVHW020758200324
774984LV00004B/445

9 781685 710644